MAPS
MYSTERY, ADVENTURE, POETRY, SUSPENSE

MAPS
MYSTERY, ADVENTURE, POETRY, SUSPENSE

CAROLYN CROOP

Copyright © Carolyn Croop.

All rights reserved. No part of this book may be reproduced in any form or by any electronic or mechanical means, including information storage and retrieval systems, without permission in writing from the publisher, except by reviewers, who may quote brief passages in a review.

ISBN: 978-1-63732-217-8 (Paperback Edition)
ISBN: 978-1-63732-218-5 (Hardcover Edition)
ISBN: 978-1-63732-216-1 (E-book Edition)

Some characters and events in this book are fictitious. Any similarity to real persons, living or dead, is coincidental and not intended by the author.

Book Ordering Information

Phone Number: 315 288-7939 ext. 1000 or 347-901-4920
Email: info@globalsummithouse.com
Global Summit House
www.globalsummithouse.com

Printed in the United States of America

CONTENTS

Chapter 1 1
Chapter 2 2
Chapter 3 4
Chapter 4 7
Chapter 5 9
Chapter 6 12
Chapter 7 14
Chapter 8 16
Chapter 9 17
Chapter 10 19
Chapter 11 21

Mirrors Of Me

Chapter 1 37
Chapter 2 38
Chapter 3 40
Chapter 4 44
Chapter 5 45
Chapter 6 47
Chapter 7 50
Chapter 8 55

Part II

Chapter 1 59
Chapter 2 62

The Promise— (First Couple)

Introduction	79
Chapter 1	83
Chapter 2	87
Chapter 3	88
Chapter 4	89
Chapter 5	92
Chapter 6	93
Chapter 7	95
Chapter 8	99
Chapter 9	101
Chapter 10	102
Chapter 11	104
Chapter 12	108
Chapter 13	111
Chapter 14	115
Chapter 15	119
Chapter 16	123

The Witness

Chapter 1	127
Chapter 2	129
Chapter 3	131
Chapter 4	133
Chapter 5	135
Chapter 6	139
Chapter 7	142
Chapter 8	143
Chapter 9	145
Chapter 10	147
Chapter 11	149
Chapter 12	151
Chapter 13	153
Chapter 14	155
Chapter 15	156
Chapter 16	157
Chapter 17	160

Chapter 18 162
Chapter 19 164
Chapter 20 168
Chapter 21 170
Chapter 22 172
Chapter 23 173
Chapter 24 175
Chapter 25 176
Chapter 26 178
Chapter 27 180
Chapter 28 182
Chapter 29 183
Chapter 30 184
Chapter 31 185
Chapter 32 186
Chapter 33 187

About the Author 189

Dedicated to my mother and Aunt Eleanor

BIRDS

I never appreciated how sweet your singing is
Until I was confined in a hospital
Unable to hear it.
Now I find its beauty
And hear your sweet chirping, caroling.
"We are all vulnerable."
It brings a reminder of life to me
That life is a mystery
That at any time
To anyone
Anything may happen.

CHAPTER 1

Islands Lost in Time

"Noble, my father always loved the water," Grayson said. "How'd you like to take an excursion?"

"I'm not sure what you mean," Noble said.

"They always said you were great at making waves. My father's dying wish was to be buried out at sea. We should take a boat trip out to sea to release my father's ashes."

Grayson and Noble lived on the East Coast of the United States. They had been best friends since childhood. They were now thirty years old, and neither was married. Grayson had a girlfriend—at least for the time being. He switched girlfriends almost as often as he changed his shirt.

Noble rarely dated. He preferred to observe situations before making any moves. Observing Grayson's dating habits kept him from dating. Noble dreamed of one day finding the right woman, but he wasn't sure what type of woman he was looking for. He hoped he would know she was the one when he met her.

CHAPTER 2

The light rain had just begun on the day Grayson and Noble were to leave on their journey. The drive to the coast was a few hundred miles. Grayson and Noble walked back and forth from the car to their apartment, packing things they needed for their trip. They were going to be taking turns driving Grayson's father's Lincoln Continental, which had been left to him in his father's will.

After Grayson's last item was packed into the car, he got into the driver's seat. Noble was still inside the apartment. Noble took time to smell the roses and was never in a hurry.

As Noble got into the passenger's seat of the car, Grayson asked, "Are we all ready?"

Noble nodded and handed Grayson a sandwich.

"Thanks, bud," Grayson said.

The two men drove through the light rain. The silver Lincoln was packed to the brim, including the urn with Grayson's father's ashes. After they had driven thirty miles, the rain let up. Soon, the sun came out. They listened to classic rock, which was their favorite. They were having a great time listening and singing along until the music stopped.

"What happened?" Noble asked.

"I don't know. The radio just stopped working. I'll pull over when I get chance." Grayson drove a few more miles, exited, and pulled into a fast-food restaurant's parking lot.

Noble took a look at the radio and the instruction manual. He was considered the smarter of the two men, although Grayson was smart as well. Neither one could figure out how to fix the radio.

"Not going the rest of the way without music," Grayson said. "Pack a radio by chance, bud?"

"I didn't have one," Noble replied.

They found a secondhand store and bought a radio that was in excellent condition.

Grayson thought it was a good opportunity to call his current girlfriend. They talked for ten minutes, which was long enough for Grayson to let Linda know things were going well.

"Who is it this week?" Noble asked.

"Noble, buddy, this is the one. I'm tellin' ya. She's the one. Her name is Linda. She's beautiful, intelligent. She's the one!"

"I'm glad for you Gray." Noble, however, took Grayson's words with a grain of salt. He had said the same things about other women. They were always the one. Noble sincerely hoped that it would work out for Grayson. They were like brothers to one another.

Grayson and Noble enjoyed the rest of their road trip, listening to music and stopping for food. It only took a few hours to get to the cottage by the ocean. Grayson's father had owned the cottage and the boat. Grayson had a large family, but his immediate family was small. Grayson's father and Barbara had divorced several years before. Grayson's sister, Sheila, was there with her husband and children. Grayson's father had left the cottage to Sheila in his will.

No one knew Grayson and Noble were there to bring Grayson's father's ashes out to sea.

Sheila reluctantly said hello to Grayson. She was extremely materialistic and bitter that she was not given the car or the same amount of money as Grayson. She was also bitter that Grayson had kept their father's ashes. Grayson's father had only shared his wish for his ashes with Grayson. Grayson and his father had been very close. Grayson would never dishonor his father. He was set to adhere to his dying wish.

The cottage had five bedrooms. Grayson's extended family visited often. His family was close, but there had been tension between Sheila and Grayson ever since their father died. Sheila felt that she deserved more than her father's will provided her even though she was given hundreds of thousands of dollars.

Grayson and Noble ate a large meal with Grayson's family before packing up the boat and heading out to sea. Eddy, Grayson's cousin, grilled lobster, burgers, and hot dogs. Barbara, Sheila, and their aunt prepared salads in the kitchen. They had a great time conversing with one another since the family had not seen each other since the funeral.

After the meal and conversations, Grayson and Noble packed the boat. Grayson called Linda and said, "I love you, baby."

Noble shook his head and said, "You've known her how long?"

Grayson replied, "She's the one. It doesn't matter."

Noble knew it was none of his business and didn't pursue the conversation.

CHAPTER 3

Grayson and Noble said their good-byes to Grayson's family before boarding the boat.

"Do you think you'll be back for dinner?" Barbara asked.

Grayson replied, "Yeah. We're only going out for a little while."

"Okay," Barbara said. "I'll see you tonight. Have fun, you two!"

Grayson started the boat and headed to the marina. He wanted a full tank of gas before they ventured out to sea. "Someone left the boat nearly on empty," Grayson said.

As they docked the boat, Grayson and Noble said hello to Denny. They had known him for a long time. He had worked at the marina since he was a teenager and was in his fifties.

Denny gave the two men a slight smile and said, "Hey. Sorry to hear about your dad, Gray."

Grayson said, "Thank you."

Denny filled their boat with gas and said, "Be careful out there today. Hear some storm may be coming through."

Grayson replied, "Only going out for a short trip, but thanks."

Shortly after they left the marina, the wind picked up and the waves increased in size.

"He was right," Noble said. "I think there's going to be a storm."

Grayson replied, "Yeah. I'm not feeling too confident about this. Let's bury the ashes and head back." Grayson stopped the boat, headed to the cabin, and picked up his father's urn. "This is it, Dad," he said. "This is where you wanted to be." Grayson walked out of the cabin with the urn in his hands.

Noble looked directly into Grayson's eyes. He knew it was a difficult moment for his friend.

"I don't want this to be a dramatic moment," Grayson said. "Bye, Dad." He poured his father's ashes into the ocean. He shed no tears. Rather, he felt a sense of completeness.

Noble placed his hand on Grayson's shoulder and said, "It's going to be all right."

Suddenly, the sky darkened, clouds rolled in, and rain began to pour down on them. They had been too caught up in the moment to prepare for the storm.

Grayson ran to the driver's seat and pointed the boat toward land, but the waves were getting bigger and moving faster. He couldn't keep it going in the right direction. There was so much turbulence that Noble was thrown out of his seat. Their heartbeats were going a mile a minute, and their adrenaline kicked in.

Noble was knocked to the floor, and Grayson lost control of the boat.

Although both were still conscious, their only concern was remaining in the boat.

Hours passed before the storm dissipated. Their heart rates slowed, and they were worn out from the adrenaline rushes. The boat was drifting since Grayson had left the boat in neutral to save gas. The men were about to fall asleep when they hit land and came to an abrupt halt.

Grayson and Noble walked out of the cabin and saw a tall stone wall that went on for miles.

"Where are we?" Noble asked.

"Hell if I know," he replied.

They checked their supplies and found the radio from the secondhand store. It was not a two-way radio, but they had a good supply of batteries. Their food supply was also very plentiful. However, they had both lost their phones. It took an hour to decide what to do next.

It was a tough decision. If they were to survive, they had to stick together.

Grayson refused to leave the boat.

"We're going to die if we just sit here and do nothing," Noble said.

Grayson wouldn't bend. He was not going to leave the boat. He hoped someone would find them there.

Noble was ready to explore the island.

"What if the barrier extends the entire island?" Grayson asked.

"What if?"

"So, you're leaving?"

"At this point, we really have no choice. We can't live on our food supply forever. We have enough for about two weeks," Noble said.

"Okay. Be careful, brother. I love you," Grayson said.

"Love you too, brother."

Noble filled a camouflage backpack with some food, a blanket, the radio, and the batteries and began walking the perimeter of the island. He was wearing tan shorts, a navy blue T-shirt, and sneakers.

The island was barren as he walked on the sandy beach. Noble's hope was beginning to fade, although his survival instinct was still strong. He figured he was at least three miles away from the boat. He sat down on the beach, ate some crackers, drank some water, and tried not to think about dying. He knew he had to remain positive in order to survive. *Why is there a wall surrounding the entire island? Where am I?* He stared up at the wall, picked up his backpack, and began walking again. He spotted an old wooden door! *Eureka!*

There was no handle on the arched door. He placed his hands on the door and began to nudge it open. He used all his force and pushed through the vines that covered the other side of the door.

CHAPTER 4

Taking small steps, Nobel walked through the vines. He saw trees, flowers, and the back of a castle. Another stone wall had been built on each side of the castle. It was not as tall as the wall surrounding the island. In the distance, he could see hills and trees. Noble was hoping to find food and water. He began walking toward the castle and heard a girl singing. He saw the most beautiful woman on a stone bench beside a flowerbed. Her hair was long and blonde, and she was wearing a long dress that looked like something from the 1400s. She continued singing, not noticing Nobel.

He waited for the young woman's song to be done before saying anything. He didn't want to startle her, but he wanted to say something. "Excuse me," he said.

The young woman jumped up from her seat and screamed.

"It's okay. It's okay. I'm not going to harm you," Noble said.

"Who are you?" she asked.

"My name is Noble. And who do I have the pleasure of meeting?"

"I'm Julia. Everyone knows me. I don't understand, Noble. Where did you come from?"

Noble replied, "The United States."

Julia looked at Noble with some confusion in her face as she began to realize how attractive he was. Noble was a good-looking man with black, curly hair and a well-built physique. His charm overpowered her. "Did you just get out of bed?" Julia asked.

"Why do you ask?" Noble responded.

"Because you're still wearing your bedtime clothing," she said.

Noble chuckled and said, "These are my shorts, and this is my T-shirt. Do you not have these types of clothing here? By the way, what are you wearing?"

"Julia? Who are you talking to?" came a woman's voice from inside the castle.

"No one," replied Julia. "I'm talking to myself."

The woman inside the castle said, "All right Julia, but don't stay outside too long. It's soon time to do your chores."

"Yes, Your Highness," Julia said.

"Do you mind if I ask who that was?" asked Noble.

"The queen," Julia replied.

Noble's eyes grew wide. "The queen? Are you serious?"

"Yes, I'm rather serious, but are you? You're wearing your evening clothes, you say you're from somewhere named United something, and you don't know who I am. Everyone knows who I am."

Noble said, "You are very correct, my dear Julia. Everyone knows who you are, including me. You are the sweet, beautiful Julia with the voice of an angel."

Julia began to blush.

"Come with me, Julia." Noble took Julia by her hand and led the way toward the door.

"Where are you taking me?" Julia asked.

"To the ocean," Noble replied.

"Ocean? What ocean? Oceans are only in storybooks," she responded.

Noble stopped to look at her. "You're serious?"

Two guards approached and said, "Stop there!"

They captured Noble and said, "Dear maiden, are you all right? Did he hurt you?"

"I'm fine," she said. "Don't hurt him."

The guards roped Noble's hands together and took him away.

CHAPTER 5

Noble was taken into the castle's dungeon and his backpack was confiscated.

The evil queen ordered Julia inside the castle. Julia was the daughter of the king and the previous queen—Queen Mary. Her father, King Gerald, had been missing from the island for years and was presumed dead. Queen Mary died of pneumonia when Julia was a child. Before his disappearance, King Gerald married Agnes. Agnes never remarried and ruled the entire land.

Although not many people liked Queen Agnes—and the queen didn't like many people—Queen Agnes liked her stepdaughter very much. It was hard not to like Julia. She was sweet, beautiful, and kind. Julia got along well with the queen, but she understood why people didn't like her. The queen was rude and overworked the laborers of the island. Much of the work on the island was farming or metalwork. The metal on the island was mostly used to make shields and suits of armor.

The queen, wearing a long gown and golden crown, sat down at a long dinner table. Queen Agnes and Julia exchanged small talk as they were served soup and main dishes.

Queen Agnes said, "I don't know why you felt it necessary to lie to me, Julia. There was a man out in the backyard talking to you earlier. I heard him, and I saw him too. What do you know about this man I speak of?"

Julia said, "I didn't talk to him very long. I just asked why he was wearing his night clothing." Julia thought Noble was handsome, kind, and mysterious.

The queen was satisfied with Julia's answer and believed that she did not know anything else.

The servants picked up the plates and bowls, and Julia and the queen went their separate ways.

The queen retreated to her bedroom, and Julia began her chores. Even though Julia was technically a princess, she was never called a princess—and she had daily chores. The evil queen had seen to it. The castle had guardsmen, knights, servants, and even a court jester.

As Julia swept the dining hall, she conversed with some of the servants. Rumors spread around the castle of the man in the dungeon. Julia knew it had to be Noble. She had to see him and make sure he was all right. She made her way down to the dungeon and saw Noble through the prison bars.

He smiled in her direction.

A guard said, "Ma'am, what brings you here?"

"I heard rumor of a man in the dungeon and that he carried with him merchandise that is yet to be identified. May I take a look at the items?"

The guard allowed Julia to see the backpack.

"I must take this with me," she said. "I must take it to the queen." She had no intentions of giving the bag to the queen.

"Hello, sir," Julia said to Noble.

"Hello, ma'am," Noble replied.

Julia ordered the guards to temporarily leave.

Noble told her about his plan to help him escape. She would bring him clothes to blend in with the people of the island and slip him the key so that he could make his getaway.

Julia agreed to the plan, having a big crush on Noble.

He told Julia about the radio and batteries and told her how it worked. "Once you have it turned on, you will hear sounds from the place where I live. Wonderful sounds. Music."

"I don't know if I should trust you," she said and gave him a wink.

When the guards returned, Julia took the backpack and told them to feed Noble. Julia then took the backpack to her room, placed the batteries inside, and turned it on. It took a few minutes to understand how it worked, but all of a sudden, she heard loud rock music!

Julia learned how to adjust the volume and turned it lower so that no one would hear it and question her. She loved the music! She had never heard anything like it. The sounds had good beats, and she liked the lyrics too. Julia was smiling and began dancing. It was as though she had discovered a hidden treasure!

There was a knock on Julia's door, and she quickly lowered the volume.

The door opened and Queen Agnes said. "Julia, dear, what on heaven's earth are you doing?"

"Um, just fluffing up the pillows after making the bed, Queen Agnes."

The queen looked at her with suspicion. "What's that noise?"

"Noise?" Julia asked. "I don't hear anything."

Queen Agnes looked at her in disbelief but ignored the sound. She had a bigger purpose for speaking to Julia. "There's rumor going on here that you spoke to the prisoner in the dungeon today. Is this true?"

Julia said, "Yes, Your Highness. It is true. I talked to the guardsmen today to make sure the prisoner was being fed."

The queen shouted, "I don't want to hear another rumor that you have been in the dungeon or near the prisoner."

"Yes, Your Highness."

Queen Agnes headed toward the door. "And brush your hair. It's looking like a rat's nest."

When the queen left, Julia pulled the radio from under her pillow and turned it off. She brushed her hair and wondered how she was going to help Noble.

CHAPTER 6

Two days later, Julia went to the dungeon. She had a servant bring a loincloth to her the previous day so she could sew something for Noble.

Noble was beginning to wonder if she had forgotten about him.

Julia was making plans to get to the dungeon without the queen's knowledge. There was no way she could get past the guards without being seen, but she decided to take the risk and hope the guardsmen would not tell anyone.

Julia opened the door leading down to the dungeon. It was dark and cold as she took each step down the stone staircase.

"Hello, my lady," said one of the guardsmen.

"Hello, sir," she said. "The queen has ordered me to bring clothes to the prisoner."

Noble was staring and listening through the prison bars.

She walked over to Noble and handed him the clothing.

"We must escape," Noble whispered.

She whispered to him that the key was tucked inside the clothes.

"Meet me here tonight," he said.

Julia was mesmerized by Noble. When she gazed into his eyes, she felt like she had been hypnotized. She agreed to meet him that night.

As the evening moved on, Noble was prepared to leave. He just needed Julia to arrive. The hours passed slowly, and Julia was nowhere in sight. Noble could not wait any longer. He was on limited time. Grayson only had a two-week food supply, and they had to figure out how to leave the island.

Noble changed into the loincloth and thought, *I'll escape from this castle and find people to help.* When he was certain the guard was not paying attention, he unlocked his cell and quietly walked past the guard.

"Get him!" the second guard shouted.

Noble ran up the stairs and out the main door. He sped across the bridge and over the moat, but two guards grabbed him.

Noble struggled to get free, but he was sent back to the dungeon.

The queen was furious and ordered Julia to her quarters immediately. "You no longer will play the role of a princess. You are hereby thought of as a servant. Going behind my back and dismissing my instructions to not enter the dungeon? You will be on servant duty for the next ten years!"

CHAPTER 7

Julia slaved day and night while Noble sat in the cold, dark dungeon. As days passed by, life at the castle went on as usual. The queen gave orders to people within the castle and on the island. She was head of the entire land, and the people obeyed.

The morning sun arose, and the birds were busy chirping in the castle's backyard. A man opened the door in the wall surrounding the island. He had long brown hair, a mustache, and a beard. He wore brown pants, a polyester shirt, and a colorful peace sign headband. Steve was there to give a letter to Julia—a letter from her father—the king.

Steve walked toward the back castle door as he looked around in awe. Opening the castle door, he stepped inside a long, dark hallway lit with candles. "Far out," Steve said. He turned the corner, and three people were scrubbing floors and dusting furniture. He tried to remain inconspicuous, but he also had a mission—to get the letter to Julia.

"Dude? Hey dude," he said to one of the servants.

Henry was sixty-six and run down by life. "Yes, sir?"

"Sir? Oh me?" Steve said. "I'm looking for a girl named Julia. I have this letter to give her. Dude. Do you know her?"

"Sir, my name is Henry. I do not know this dude you speak of, but I do know Julia. Queen Mary and King Gerald's daughter is now a slave."

"Henry, man, can you get this letter to her?"

Henry agreed, and Steve handed the letter to him. "I'm just going to do a little wandering, man, but thanks a lot." Steve found a suit of armor, wandered over the bridge, and walked past the guards. He came across a horse tied to a tree about fifty feet from the castle and used the horse as his means of transportation.

Steve thought his suit of armor was "out of this world." And it was in a way. Though Steve was also from another world. You see, there was more than one island lost in time. Steve came from an island that was lost in the 1960s. Nothing on the island had advanced further than the 1960s.

And Julia's island was lost in the 1400s. Nothing had advanced since that timeframe either.

The king lived on the island that was lost in the 1960s. Many years prior, he had found a way to leave the island—and the queen. It hurt his heart to leave Julia behind, but the queen was overbearing and powerful. She controlled the entire land and the king.

CHAPTER 8

Steve rode the horse into town. He had no particular mission other than to explore. He found a place to tie up the horse so that he could wander on foot. He saw a sign for a tailor and entered the shop in hopes of finding something more appropriate to wear.

"Groovy," Steve said as he observed the merchandise.

The tailor was busy sewing and didn't even look up at Steve.

"Hey man," Steve said. "You willing to barter with me?"

The tailor looked up, and Steve asked about exchanging his suit of armor for a loincloth.

The tailor agreed, but he was not very friendly. In fact, no one in town was very friendly because Queen Agnes overworked everyone on the island. However, the tailor also gave Steve some extra money. After all, a suit of armor was worth much more than loincloth.

Steve found a bakery since it had been a long time since he had eaten. That day, he met the tailor, the baker, a painter, a gardener, a shoemaker, and a mason. The mason told Steve all about the evil queen, Julia, and William.

William was the town's banker. A prearranged marriage between William and Julia was set for the following year.

CHAPTER 9

While Steve was wandering the island, Julia was working hard at the castle. She had retreated to her room for the night and heard a knock on her door. A servant brought her a letter—though it was inside a paper envelope—something she had never seen before. "What is this?" Julia asked.

"Sir Steve handed this to me. He said it's from the king to you, Julia."

Julia grabbed the letter from the servant. "My father is dead." She shut the door. Julia stood by the door, looked at the envelope, and slowly stepped over to her bed. "To Julia" was written on the outside of the envelope. She noticed the flap on the envelope and wondered what it was for. She pulled the letter out of the envelope and began reading:

My dear sweet daughter, Julia,

I miss you so dearly. I have much to explain. There is another world outside the wall. And an ocean. The world is bigger than you know. You live on an island, Julia, that is ruled by the queen. She works people to their death. The ocean is bright blue water. It is enormous. Boats travel on the ocean. That is how this letter found you. I am the king of the other island. We have moved through time. We are highly advanced and educated. There—where you are—only a few have the opportunity to be educated.

I wish I knew a way to rescue you from that terrible place. Have you married William yet? Are you doing all right? Oh, Julia, I wish I knew the answers to my questions. I write this letter to let you know that I am alive—though do not let that be known. I love you, my princess. And I miss you dearly.

Love,
Father

Julia lifted her pillow and pulled out the radio. She had complete faith and trust in her father's words. She believed there was a world outside the wall. After all, the radio was proof of that. Julia had only met William a few times. She was not impressed. She found him to be a bit of a snob.

Julia turned on the radio and heard a breaking news announcement. Two men had been lost at sea. The radio broadcasters were interviewing a man named Jeremy.

"Please help," he said. "Noble and Grayson—they need to be found."

CHAPTER 10

After Steve heard about the prearranged marriage for William and Julia, he knew he had to get back to the castle to stop it. As he wandered toward the outdoor guards, his hands were immediately shackled. He was sent to the dungeon.

Steve and Noble met in the dungeon prison and got to know one another. Steve told Noble about the island where he lived, and Noble told Steve about the even bigger world.

"Wow, so totally far out," said Steve. Steve told Noble about the prearranged marriage.

Noble had to find a way to rescue Julia.

Steve pulled a lighter out of his pocket.

Noble's eyes lit up. He knew it would be the tool to make their great escape.

Noble used Steve's lighter to create a fire in the prison. When the guardsmen saw smoke, they immediately opened the prison door to let Steve and Noble out. Steve and Noble fought the two guards and ran up to the main area of the castle.

At midnight, no one was around. They roamed the castle and found Julia's room.

Noble opened the door and woke Julia with a kiss. "Hurry," Noble said. "We don't have time to wait." He grabbed Julia's hand, and they walked to the beauty of the ocean.

Julia's eyes lit up wide.

Steve's boat was anchored right outside the wooden door.

Noble asked Steve if he would drive them over to Grayson's boat.

"Definitely, brother." When he tried to start the boat, he discovered it was out of gas. They began to walk to Grayson's boat.

Noble and Julia held hands.

"Where are we going?" asked Julia.

Noble replied, "To the boat … where my friend Grayson is." They walked a few miles, both smiling along the way. They were falling in love.

Steve was following them.

Noble spotted the boat. "Grayson! Grayson!" Noble ran toward the boat.

Grayson stepped out to look and said, "Where the hell have you been?"

Noble introduced Julia and Steve to Grayson. "Grayson, man, you wouldn't believe it if I told you. How much food and water do you have left?"

Grayson replied, "Enough for one more day. The bad news is there's a gas leak in the boat? I'd say you've lost it, Noble—except I see these two people—or maybe I'm hallucinating too."

The four sat inside the boat and talked. After an hour, they heard a helicopter hovering above them. It dropped a ladder to them. Julia was scared, but Noble calmed her down and told her that the helicopter was there to rescue them.

The pilot flew toward the United States.

"How did you know we were there?" Grayson asked.

The pilot replied, "A man named Jeremy insisted that two men were trapped on an island on the outskirts of the United States. I'll be reporting back about what I saw there. I never knew that island was there. It has never shown up on my radar, and that was some wall surrounding it. It looked like something out of a fairytale."

CHAPTER 11

The emergency lights suddenly displayed inside the helicopter. The pilot had to make an emergency landing. He was flying over the United States and made an emergency landing in a large field. His communication systems also failed.

They got out of the helicopter and walked to a small town. The pilot went inside a gas station to use the phone, and Noble and Grayson talked. They were a few miles from Grayson's family cottage. They thanked the pilot and walked to the cottage.

At the cottage, Grayson's family and Linda greeted them. Noble introduced Steve and Julia to Grayson's family and Linda. Linda had been at the cottage for two weeks during Noble and Grayson's disappearance. Grayson knew that Linda was the one for him.

They all hugged and talked. Barbara was overwhelmed but so happy that they had survived the ordeal.

Grayson said, "Where's Sheila?"

Barbara said, "She's reading Dylan a bedtime story and tucking him in. Go see her, Grayson."

Grayson walked to Dylan's bedroom and saw his sister reading to her son. "And the island was forever lost in time with Queen Agnes ruling the land. Julia and William then married."

JOURNEY OF THE MIND
BOOK 1 (PART I)

As I got into bed
And fell asleep
The dream within my head
Became rather deep.
A journey into the mind
I had begun
The real world I left behind
To where there was no moon or sun.
I started at the spinal cord,
Which brings information in.
I was in a tiny boat and oared
A brain journey I was about to begin.
I rowed upward through the brain
Where there stood a control panel.
I had to refrain
From pressing different channels.
I was in the brain stem, which keeps the heart beating.
It keeps circulation going.
Digestion is not depleting,
For it keeps digestion flowing.
The basic functions are close
To the spinal cord.
I then found a map lined in rows.
Though in reality I had snored,
I paddled on upward
After visiting three parts of the brain stem.
As I traveled onward,
I waved good-bye to them.

The three parts I visited were
The medulla oblongata, the pons,
And the midbrain there.

As I rowed quietly by several swans,
I actually traveled behind
Into the cerebellum.
There, I did find
The beating of a drum.
For the Cerebellum gives you
Motor memory and body control.
This is true.
It will guide you to run or stroll.
Suddenly, I received
A sensory-nerve telegram.
I perceived
That my leg was in a jam.
My leg was tangled
In my blankets and sheets.
I then signaled
To move my feet.
Next, I rowed up to
The thalamus on top of the brain stem.
It is true.
This part is a gem.
The thalamus is like a mailroom.
It sorts data and sends it slow
Slow—not fast—I would assume
To where it needs to go.
All of a sudden, just then,
There was a strong current.
That was when
I forgot to say what I meant.
My boat sank down
Into the hypothalamus.
I almost drowned
But hopped onto a tour bus.

JOURNEY OF THE MIND
BOOK 1 (PART II)

So there I was
Just me on a tour bus.
And it was because
I got lost in the hypothalamus.
Just then I felt a chill.
The hypothalamus maintains temperature.
As the bus drove up a hill,
I thought—what an adventure!
Next stop, the cerebrum,
Where it makes sense of data coming in.
Suddenly, I heard the beating of a drum.
As the bus went for a spin,
In my view were billions of neurons,
Which are nerve cells.
If I counted them, it would take eons.
Just then, the sound of bells.
Bells rang each time
There was a connection between neurons
Clocks, too, would chime.
The colors were all neon.
In the cerebrum,
There is a left and right
Connected by nerves called corpus callosum.
The brain inside looked like night.
The bus first went to the left side.
I saw math and logic on the walls.
There weren't really walls at all.
Next, the tour bus went right

Where there was a mirror
Within my sight.
I saw it clear.

The right side of the brain
Is for facial recognition.
I then saw a train
At a station.
Before I hopped on,
I looked in the mirror.
I had begun
To see myself clear.
Yes, in the mirror was me.
But inside this brain?
Could this be?
Could this brain be mine to see?

JOURNEY OF THE MIND
BOOK 1 (PART III)

I hopped on the train, traveling down to the basil ganglia.
I saw a bunch of nuclei
In this brain area.
(I tell the truth and do not lie.)
Nuclei or nucleus are neurons
Next to each other
For the reason
Of the same function as one another.
Here there is inhibition
And excitatory responses too.
I then saw another train station
Within my view.
The complex interaction here
Of the responses between neurons
Controls a lot of motor control there.
The interactions move like pawns.
I then saw a door
That said: Do Not Enter—Stop!
I wondered what for.
A tear from within my eye then dropped.
Parkinson's disease, it said
Underneath the sign.
I hope by seeing what I read
I would turn out fine.
The train moved up to the cerebral cortex,
Which is about 80 percent of the brain.
I then got a text
While on the train.
The text that I received

Was somehow from me.
I believed
There was a reason for this dream.

The map of this section—
The cerebral cortex part—
Was broken into four selections.
I wondered where to start
The first part was the frontal lobe,
Which is the boss of one's brain.
This adventure was like touring the globe
From inside my brain on a train.
Suddenly, I began to cry.
It's emotional control here.
I would then try
To get out of here.
The train moved to the parietal lobe.
It's where I react to my environment.
Within my brain, I probed,
Displaying great excitement.
A lot of neurons come here
From a sensory input also.
To each other they share.
(I then adjusted my pillow.)
The train then went to
The occipital lobe
Where I see things in my view.
This trip was like a space probe.
Next, the temporal lobe—
Important in memory, language, and hearing.
Suddenly, I wondered about this probe
And wondered who was steering.
I looked for the train's conductor
But I saw no one—
Not even an instructor.
Oh, well—this was fun!

JOURNEY OF THE MIND
BOOK 1 (PART IV)

Buzz—the alarm clock sounded.
My adventure—finished.
Though I was astounded,
My lack of knowledge diminished.
I had learned a little something
About myself within my brain.
To myself, I could bring
Thoughts I would not refrain.
For what I failed to say
Was how beautiful it was there.
It looked like night—not day.
Though lights were everywhere,
I then realized
What an amazing mind I had.
Myself, I then idealized.
Of me, I was in high demand.
My brain is really smart,
But when I dream tonight,
I will travel to my heart
Where love lights up the night.

JOURNEY OF THE MIND
BOOK 2 (PART I)

I went to work one day,
Following my journey of the mind.
The day before yesterday,
I had met a man gentle and kind.
It felt like love at first sight.
Though I didn't give him the time of day,
I used all my mind's might
To keep him far away.
Though at work that day.
He handed me a note
It said, "How about Friday?"
"You're beautiful," he wrote.
The day was Wednesday.
I tried to keep him out of my mind.
Though I agreed to Friday
Only because he was so kind.
For I was done with men and dating.
Thus, I hadn't dated in years.
I was awaiting
To abolish all my fears.
I had been mistreated
By men in my life.
They had lied and cheated
One never even told me he had a wife.
Later that day, I took a train
And I went home to bed.
I wondered about my dream of my brain
And kept my date out of my head.

I fell asleep soon after
And was about to travel to my heart.
I muttered something with laughter.
My journey was about to start.

JOURNEY OF THE MIND
BOOK 2 (PART II)

I went via boat
Through my heart.
I thought about Russell's note
Though, from my mind, I was now far apart.
The heart is the size of a fist.
It is the most important muscle.
Now here is the twist:
I think I'm in love with this new man named Russell.
The reason why
I think this is true
Is because when I try
Not to think of him, I'm blue.
I traveled to the right and left ventricle and atrium
(The four major chambers).
Inside my heart, I felt like an alien.
(By the way, my name is Amber.)
I first went to the right
Side of my heart.
Nothing was in my sight.
For here is where feelings play their part.
Suddenly, I had trouble breathing there
For the right side receives low oxygen.
Oxygen is carried through blood here,
Though I will refer to it as a sea in a dungeon.
This low oxygen
Is received for veins everywhere.
In this heart dungeon,
I felt as though I really cared.
My boat was pumped into

The pulmonary artery
My heart was then stolen—it's true.
There had been a burglary.

For my heart was no longer mine.
I did not own it.
I then saw a neon sign
Saying, "Russell owns all—not just a bit."
I then went into the lungs
Where the sea gets air again.
I then had begun
To return to the heart within.
I returned to the left side
Where the reoxygenated sea returns.
My boat just about capsized.
I became a bit concerned.
I was pumped up to the aorta,
But I got stuck
In this aorta area.
"Just my luck."
A sign said, "Go no farther
For the sea here will part.
Don't bother
To leave the heart."

JOURNEY OF THE MIND
BOOK 2 (PART III)

What was I to do?
I was stuck in my heart.
Love was something new.
Was Russell also in my mind's part?
I then turned over in bed
To the other side.
I began a journey back into my head
For my heart and head must abide.
They must both abide
By my rule of love—
To both align
The heart and head above.
Suddenly, I woke up
For a brief instant
To fill my water cup.
In a few minutes,
Though it took a lot longer
Than I had thought,
My snoring became stronger.
I was somewhat distraught
For I was not in my home.
I was in Russell's residence
Though I was all alone
And in only my presence.
He had stolen my heart,
But it was nowhere in sight
This love in my heart would start
To light up the night.
Thoughts in my head
Became more clear.

For I was home in my bed.
My boat I then steered
Into my mind
Where neurons moved fast.
My heart and head were aligned.
Love I found at last.

MIRRORS OF ME

CHAPTER 1

The war hit suddenly. Cities and towns throughout the United States of America blasted emergency alarms, and televisions and radios broadcasted emergency sounds. Cellular phones beeped with a special alert code and displayed notification that the president would be making an important announcement in the next five minutes. Notice of the president's speech was also broadcast via Internet, television, and radio.

Five minutes later, the president spoke from the Oval Office. He said, "Americans everywhere, we are at war— with one another. Today marks the official start of a civil war within the country between the West and the East. As you are aware, there has been an onset of confliction between the two areas. It is imminent that each individual remain or return to his or her homeland—West or East. I am not mandating that you stay inside your homes at this time, although it is highly recommended. The police, sheriffs, FBI, SWAT units, and military personnel are on the scenes in every city and town across the country to help ensure each person's safety. Washington, DC, is the only neutral place. This area will not choose a side to preference over the other. God bless America."

Broadcasters stepped in to recap what the president had said and to help make sense of it all. Panic filled the streets. Fights broke out. People rushed to return to their homes.

CHAPTER 2

Onalee had vast pride in her country—the good old United States of America. Only twenty-four years of age, she had big dreams. Onalee was raised and lived in New York. Her personality was happy-go-lucky and easygoing. Throughout her life, she would talk enthusiastically about her plans for the future. She dreamed of getting married, becoming an author, and living in California. A dream of marriage was not unusual, but becoming an author and living in California surprised the people in her life because she had never written anything—and she had never even been anywhere on the West Coast. The farthest she had ever been was Ohio. Onalee had made a promise to David—her closest friend—that she would one day make a trip to Missouri where he resided.

Onalee and David had met each other on an Internet website three years prior to the start of the war. David was unlike any man she had ever met. Most of the men she met through the Internet wanted to know more about her physical appearance than her intellect. Onalee had always valued her intelligence. She wanted to be known for her brains and not solely for her beauty. David was the first man to show Onalee respect for both.

Onalee was five foot two and weighed less than 120 pounds. She had blonde, curly hair and had good taste in clothes. Although she didn't have what it took to be a model, she had been called "pretty" on many occasions. Her intelligence was slightly above average, but her high school math teacher questioned whether she was actually a genius. Onalee grasped mathematical concepts with ease. Mr. Carpenter, her math teacher, only realized it toward the end of her senior year.

Onalee had placed more effort on her social life than on schoolwork. She rarely studied and slid by with passing grades. One month before she was to graduate, her guidance counselor told Onalee that she would not be graduating if she did not pass her final math examination. Onalee spent the remainder of school year studying math in her spare time.

After the results of the examinations were in, Mr. Carpenter was astounded. Onalee passed the examination with flying colors. She even answered the most difficult and challenging question correctly. Mr. Carpenter felt a sense of pride for her—and sadness that he had discovered Onalee's intelligence too late.

Onalee chose to work instead of attending college. She was a hard worker and worked at various different minimum-wage jobs until she was twenty-four. She enjoyed earning money and saved half of what she earned. The money she saved was intended for pursuing her dreams.

CHAPTER 3

When the news of Civil War 2 broke out, Onalee was devastated. There was uncertainty among everyone around her. Some people stated that the United States would probably turn into two countries, while others were more hopeful that everything would be resolved. Onalee swayed more toward resolution.

It had been a month since the start of the war, and the crisis had calmed down. In some ways, the situation looked worse. By that time, everyone was in the West or East. People were no longer panicked, but they were growing more and more concerned that a quick resolution was impossible. Everyone in the United States was required to wear dog tags with a unique number and a "W" for those in the West or an "E" for those in the East. Law enforcement and military personnel were commanded to remain impartial, but they also wore the dog tags.

Onalee read the news on the Internet daily. One article told stories about people moving to the opposite side. It talked about individuals and families with relatives or loved ones on the other coast. Edward Olin and Elise Winslow had a four-year long-distance relationship. Both were in love with each other, and they weren't sure if they could live apart any longer. Edward took it upon himself to leave Oregon and go to Vermont with Elise. Federal officials captured him right after he crossed the dividing line.

The army commander convinced the president to build a wall in the middle of the country. The president was aware of the severity of the issue and ordered federal constructionists in DC to build the wall. The president didn't stop there. He met with CEOs of phone and Internet companies to prevent any communication between the two sides. This took two months to complete.

In the meantime, Onalee was determined to cross the border into California. Although there was no particular person she was trying to find, she had a strong sense that California was where she needed to be. Not knowing about the president's plans for a wall and communication restrictions, Onalee was ready to set out for California. She felt it was time to go. Fear was the catalyst for her decision. Onalee thought she might never see the West if the United States continued fighting or became two countries. She snuck out of her mother's house and started on her journey.

"In Civil War 1, they rode horses. At least I got a car," Onalee said as she drove. At each state line she crossed, her dog tags were checked. She began to realize that she might not be able to get through. Her New York plates would stick out like a sore thumb.

By the time Onalee reached Kentucky, she was exhausted. She found a hotel to stay for the night. There were three hotels, and she chose the one that looked best.

As Onalee walked up to the counter, a friendly old woman said, "May I help you?"

Onalee asked if there was a vacant room for the night.

Betty told her that there was only one king-sized room left.

Onalee said, "I'll take it." She brought her bags to her room and fell asleep.

Onalee's original plan was to surprise David at his apartment. She thought it would be a nice gesture since David lived along the route to California. The next day, she started to rethink her idea. The reality of her dilemma moved to the front of her brain. She could not figure out how she was going to get past the security checkpoints on the West while wearing her dog tags. She needed David's help. They typically talked at least three times per week, but they had not talked since Onalee left New York.

The communication systems had not yet been altered, and Onalee decided to break the news to him that she was on her way to his home. She started out by texting: "Is it okay to call now?"

David received the text and called Onalee.

She told David that she had left New York and was in a hotel in Kentucky. "I'm a little stuck," Onalee said.

"You are crazy enough to take a trip like this on your own, aren't you?" he said.

Onalee told David about her dilemma with the security checkpoints, but he assured her that there were no checkpoints in the West.

David told her to leave her car and phone at the Kentucky-Mississippi border and cross the border by foot. "There's a bus station five minutes from there. Hop on a bus to Missouri. The bus station here is a ten-minute walk from my apartment. There's only one problem, Onalee."

"Oh no. What's wrong?" she asked.

"My dad doesn't like you because you're from the East," he said. David lived with his father. It was just the two of them since his mother passed away. "Don't take it personally, Onalee. He doesn't like anyone from the East."

It was difficult for Onalee to not take it personally. Even though she was a strong-willed woman, she was very sensitive. She told David not to worry.

David worried that his dad might even try to shoot her.

Onalee drove to the border and left her car and phone in a church parking lot. Before she got out of her car, a middle-aged man approached. He had a gray beard, a mustache, ratty jeans, and a flannel shirt. He motioned for Onalee to roll down her window. She felt a slight sense of fear but rolled down her window.

The man said, "I see you're from New York."

Onalee shook her head and said, "Yes, I am."

The man said, "There used to be a bar named New York down the road."

She could tell that people from the area rarely came across anyone from New York. Onalee told him that was interesting. She was hoping he wouldn't ask her where she was headed, but he just smiled, told her to have a nice day, and walked back to his car. Onalee waited for him to drive away, got out of her car, and walked across the border.

Five minutes later, she reached the bus station and bought a ticket to Missouri. She found a family restaurant, sat down, and began thinking about David's father. No one she encountered in the West knew she was from the East—except for David and his father.

For the remainder of the day, Onalee scoped out David's apartment. As evening approached, she began her journey to David's apartment. Onalee waited across the street until she was confident that David's father was asleep.

The lights in David's one-bedroom apartment were out. David slept on the living room couch, and his dad used the bedroom. Onalee picked up three stones and threw them at the front window. A minute later, the front door opened.

David had a bag packed as he greeted Onalee with a big hug.

"Okay, David," said Onalee. "It's your turn to take over. I'm out of ideas. Where do we go from here?"

"To California!" David exclaimed.

Onalee said, "How? You don't drive."

"But you do." David handed over his father's car keys.

Onalee had a huge smile on her face. David truly was her best friend. He had come through for her.

"Let's go," David whispered.

David and Onalee started on their journey to California.

CHAPTER 4

"I don't understand, David. Why are there no security checkpoints out here?"

David said, "I don't understand why you're so scared. Listen, Onalee. The East is stringent, but in the West, we're not as uptight."

Onalee said, "We're not uptight, David. We just care about our citizens' safety a little bit more than you do out here." Onalee realized she had fallen into the same trap as the rest of the country.

David simply viewed his best friend as independent in her thoughts and ways.

Onalee said that she was sorry about how she came across, and David said there was no need to apologize.

Over the course of the next few days, David and Onalee's relationship remained as a friendship. David had his sights set on an Asian woman he had met on the Internet. Onalee was too focused on her independence to be involved with any man, but they cared for one another.

They were alerted that the president would be speaking in several minutes. David and Onalee listened to the car radio as the president spoke. The president's communications plan was effective immediately. He also announced the wall.

David told Onalee to return to the East before the wall went up, but she refused to take his advice.

CHAPTER 5

After a few days, money was tight. David suggested stopping in Las Vegas. Onalee wasn't surprised since he told her all the time about his scratch-off lottery tickets. He played the lottery at every chance he had. Onalee told him they had to continue to California as planned.

David said, "Remind me about your reason for wanting to get to California."

"That doesn't even deserve a response. We've known each other for three years, and all along, I have told you the reason."

David said, "Because you just want to?"

"Not just because I want to," Onalee said. "There's a lot more to it than that."

"Then what is it?" David asked.

"It has been a dream of mine since I was a kid."

"But why is it so important, Onalee? Answer that. There's got to be more to it than that."

Onalee pulled off into a strip mall parking lot, bowed her head for a moment, and said, "My grandmother died four years ago."

"I know. You told me that when we met on the Internet. What does that have to do with traveling to California?"

"My grandmother never fulfilled any of her dreams. She worked for years at a job she didn't even like. She got pregnant at seventeen and married my grandfather at eighteen. She wasn't in love with him. She was madly in love with someone else, but she married my grandfather because she felt it was the right thing to do. She never wanted to be a mother at such a young age. She had dreams of being an actress and moving to Hollywood. Instead she spent her life raising five children. My grandmother never even traveled anywhere for vacation. She spent every penny she earned on the basics—food, shelter, and clothing for all of us. There was never any extra money. She never went out for a nice meal or even to the movies. Her everyday life consisted of simply making ends meet and getting by. Then she died. I have always dreamed of going to California. And there's no reason. It is just a dream. I'm not going to die with my unfulfilled dreams buried with me like my grandmother did. My dreams are going to become reality."

David said that he understood even though he still thought she was a bit crazy. He spotted a sub shop and said, "Let's get something to eat."

They ordered submarine sandwiches, but when it came time to pay, David had barely enough. Onalee looked at his wallet, which had only a few dollars left. She looked up at David with great concern.

When they returned to the car to eat, David said, "Now what do you think about a stop in Vegas?"

Onalee realized they had no other choice. It was the only option to try to win more money. "What do we do about gas money?" she asked.

David pulled a brand-new credit/debit card from his wallet. He had always told Onalee that he received credit card offers in the mail, and she always told him to refuse them. David was a spender even though he never had enough money to get by. He relied on his father to help him out every month, but his father didn't have much money either.

"How much money is on the card?" she asked.

"It's never been used. There's a five hundred-dollar credit line."

They looked at each other and smiled.

"Okay, David. You're getting your way. Off to Vegas it is," Onalee said.

CHAPTER 6

"David, who are you texting?" Onalee asked.

"My dad," he said.

"You shouldn't be speaking to anyone. You're not telling him where we are, right?"

David replied, "No, but he wants to know where I am. He told me his car has been stolen. I told him I'm all right. I said I went out for a walk. He doesn't even know you're with me."

Onalee responded, "Good. Keep it that way. You know the authorities can track us through your cell phone, right?"

"I know, but my dad won't go to the authorities. He thinks I'm out on a walk."

"For now, he thinks you're out on a walk. What happens tomorrow?"

David hadn't thought that far ahead.

An hour later, Onalee and David arrived in Las Vegas. They were in great need of a shower and a change of clothes, but neither of them had anything else to wear. They decided not to concern themselves with that and went inside the first casino they came across.

Onalee felt out of place in the Royal Grand Casino. People were dressed in expensive clothing and were all groomed.

David focused on the slot machines. He spotted an automatic teller machine and used his credit card to get three hundred dollars.

Onalee told him not to use all of the money.

He told her he wouldn't spend it all, but he played the slot machines for an hour until he had only twenty dollars left.

Onalee stood by his side, watching him the entire time. She became more nervous each time he put money in the machine. "You're done." Onalee took David's hand, led him to a poker table, and asked David for the twenty dollars.

David said, "You can't play that."

Onalee said, "Watch me."

David pulled out his wallet and handed Onalee the twenty dollars. She placed the money on the table and shocked everyone.

David wasn't even aware that she knew how to play poker, but Onalee had a vast interest in many different things. She sometimes watched videos to gain knowledge on various subjects—ranging from physics to gambling.

Onalee won several rounds, and a large crowd formed around her. By the time the managers and security officers arrived, Onalee had won $2 million. The managers and security officers led her to an office and gave Onalee ten thousand in cash and a check.

Onalee spotted David on her way out of the office.

"Great job!" David said.

They got back to the car, and David asked how she was able to win.

Onalee said, "The law of probability. I learned about it in math class in high school."

Onalee took the money out of her purse and gave half of it to David.

He thanked her and said that he wanted to go inside for one last chance at the slot machines. Onalee advised him that his idea was a bad choice, but he insisted on playing one last time. He said he wouldn't be in there long.

Onalee remained in the car. As David walked toward the casino, two men mugged him. They took his million dollars and drove away. David rushed back to his father's car and got into the passenger seat. He was devastated, but Onalee reminded him that they still had a million dollars. They discussed the situation for a few moments and decided to continue on to California.

After two blocks, she stopped at a red light.

David looked over at the car next to them and saw the thieves. Without hesitation, David opened the glove compartment, pulled out his father's pistol, and pointed it at the men.

Onalee shouted, "No, David. Don't! Remember what Mahatma Gandhi said? An eye for an eye makes the whole world blind."

David was eager to pull the trigger and shoot, but he thought about what she had said as the light turned green. He knew Onalee was right. The quote even made him chuckle because he knew of no one else who would repeat a famous quote in a time of desperation. Small idiosyncrasies like that were what made Onalee his best friend.

The two thieves sped off as Onalee drove slowly through the green light.

David put the gun back into the glove compartment. "I didn't even know you had a gun in there," she said.

"It's my father's gun," he said. "And, by the way, Onalee, you were right."

Onalee pulled over at a convenience store to buy a map. "Need anything while I'm in there?" she asked.

He replied, "Am energy drink please."

While walking back to the car, she saw David in the driver's seat. Onalee got into the passenger's seat and handed David his drink. The two sat in the car while Onalee read the map. She figured out the routes they needed to take and said, "Okay, time to switch seats."

David wanted to drive the rest of the way.

Onalee said, "No way, David. You don't have your license." David had, for a brief time, lost the privilege of having a driver's license because he was late in renewing it.

He explained that her license wasn't even valid in the West.

"It's valid everywhere in the United States," she exclaimed.

"Not anymore," David said. "Not since the start of the Civil War."

Onalee realized that David was right. "Not too fast though."

David sped down the street.

After fifteen minutes, Onalee gave into her emotions and decided that the adventure was thrilling! She told him which roads to take as they raced down the highway.

CHAPTER 7

David and Onalee drove from Nevada to California in one day.

Onalee was excited when they finally made it to her dream destination! She couldn't wait to go sightseeing and explore the state.

David pulled along the road, and they took a nap. When they awoke, they ate potato chips and crackers.

Onalee told David to start the car and head up the road. "Turn right!" Onalee said.

David turned into a motel parking lot. "Why are we here?"

"So we can both take showers," she said.

"Why not a luxury hotel, Miss Big Bucks?"

"I'm hoping we can just pay for a room with no questions asked. And if they need our identification, you can give them yours and tell them that I'm your wife. They don't need to know that I'm from the East."

David said, "Good plan." He walked into the run-down motel, and Onalee stayed in the car.

"I see you have Missouri plates," said the clerk. "What brings you out this way?"

David said that he had just been to Las Vegas to get married and that he and his wife were in California for their honeymoon.

"Aw, that's sweet," the clerk said. "But why are you choosing this place for a honeymoon?"

David explained that they had lost most of their money in Vegas.

"Room eight. Here's the key," the clerk said, never even checking David's identification.

As David walked back out to the car, a guilty feeling surfaced. There had been no reason for his lies. After all, the clerk never even checked his identification. "What's become of me?"

Onalee said, "What do you mean by that?"

David placed his hand on her shoulder and said, "We're good to go. The clerk never even asked for our identification. Here's the key."

Onalee said, "Great! But, I still don't know what you meant."

David said he would explain after they got settled in the room.

David placed his bag on the bed, and Onalee didn't hesitate as she walked into the bathroom for her shower. David watched television and rested.

Onalee read the newspaper while David showered. As she glanced at the headlines, it became apparent that she was in more danger than she realized. Thousands of people from the East had been hunted down and killed. As she flipped over the page, she spotted a picture of her favorite band. The band would be performing in San Jose that same day. There was no doubt that Onalee would find a way to attend.

David walked into the room, and Onalee asked to explain his earlier statement.

David told Onalee about his guilty feelings. "What's your plan now?"

"Adventureland Amusement Park in San Jose."

"Why?" he asked.

"Because it's fun, David. Life is about having fun!"

David drove toward San Francisco.

"I said San Jose, David—not San Francisco."

"I know, Onalee, but I'm a bit lost."

Onalee got the map out again, but she discovered it was not a map of the entire state. "I guess we need to buy another map," she said.

"No, we'll get there without one," he said.

Onalee asked David if he knew where they were.

David had no clue where they were.

Onalee said, "Great."

David pulled over to talk, but Onalee got out of the car to wave down another car.

Within five minutes, a car stopped. A friendly woman asked if she needed help.

Onalee said, "Yes, do you know the way to San Jose?"

The woman gave Onalee the directions to San Jose.

David asked, "Where's the nearest church?"

Onalee was stunned because David rarely talked to strangers, and the people who knew him always described David as antisocial, according to what he had told Onalee during their previous Internet chats. Onalee was also hopeful that David wasn't planning on marrying her. She had dreams of marriage, but she didn't want to fulfill that dream yet.

The woman pointed to a community church on the top of the hill. David thanked her, and they drove up the hill.

"What are we here for?" asked Onalee.

David responded, "To repent and pray for our salvation."

Onalee knew little about church and God. She had not been raised in the church.

David, on the other hand, attended church every Sunday before his mother died. He had been educated about Christ and the Bible at an early age. David's mother had even been one of the Sunday school teachers at his family's church.

David led the way into the church, and Onalee followed.

"I'm afraid I won't know the right gestures," Onalee said.

David looked confused and asked what she meant.

Onalee said that she didn't know when to make the sign of the cross or when to shake people's hand and say, "Peace be with you."

David explained that it was not a Catholic church and that she didn't need to know any particular gestures.

Onalee felt a sense of relief and asked, "So this isn't a Christian church?"

David replied that it was a Christian church—but not a Catholic church.

Onalee was still confused because she knew the Catholic faith was Christian.

David said, "There are different denominations under the Christian faith. Christianity is like a heading, and underneath the heading are Catholic, Episcopalian, Protestant, Methodist, and so on. And to be Christian means that you believe in Jesus Christ."

"That makes a lot of sense. So, which denomination is this church?"

David replied, "This is a community church. It means that it welcomes all denominations of the Christian faith."

"I see," said Onalee.

A minister stood at the podium and began to speak. She started by welcoming all visitors and newcomers and went on to recite two verses from the Bible. It took twenty minutes for the minister to speak about her interpretation of the verses.

Onalee asked David when they were going to repent and pray.

Right after she asked, the minister stated that there would be a moment of silence for repentance and prayer. David and Onalee prayed to God and apologized to him for their sins. The minister continued with the rest of the sermon and talked about Jesus.

Onalee asked David about the difference between God and Jesus.

David was a bit stunned that Onalee was that poorly educated. However, he didn't make any judgments of her because of her lack of religious knowledge. He explained to Onalee that Jesus is the Son of God and that Jesus is God.

Onalee was beginning to understand.

When it was over, David and Onalee left the church with a great sense of peace. David asked Onalee if she'd like to do some of the driving, but she said that she was better at giving directions. David followed the directions to San Jose. Upon their arrival in the city, they stopped at a gas station and asked for directions to the amusement park.

David parked by the main entrance of the amusement park. Onalee was anxious to ride the roller coaster, but David had his sights set on food. They bought ice cream and bottled water. Onalee was ready to ride the roller coaster, but David was afraid of heights. Onalee talked him onto the ride. He actually had the time of his life! They ended up riding every ride within the park.

At four thirty, Onalee led David over to the performing arts center. She confessed the real reason why they were at the amusement park.

David was excited since he liked the band as well. They got front-row seats and cheered as the first song began. David and Onalee knew every song. When the concert was over, the band announced that the people in rows one and two were welcome to go backstage to meet and greet them.

David and Onalee introduced themselves to the band, and David said, "She never stops talking about you."

The lead singer, Adam, invited them to his mansion. He gave them his address, but he forgot to tell them the date and time for their invitation. Adam was distracted by other fans and was unable to talk more to David and Onalee.

David and Onalee decided to go on more rides. They rode the roller coaster three more times, and then they rode the bumper cars, tilt-a-whirl, and even the merry-go-round.

David and Onalee were exhausted when they got to the car.

David combed the area for a hotel.

"There's no point in checking into a hotel," Onalee said. "It would be a sin."

David knew she was right even though he was exhausted. He asked if she could take over the driving while he took a nap.

Onalee drove as David slept. She was exhausted, but she wanted to drive to Adam's mansion to mingle some more.

By the time Onalee reached the mansion, her thoughts were racing and unclear. She was having a mental breakdown, but she was unaware of it.

Onalee parked outside Adam's house and took off her clothes. She said, "I'm close to understanding Jesus."

Without warning, a group of three men told Onalee to put her clothes back on. They handcuffed David and Onalee. None of the men were wearing uniforms. One of the men opened the back of a large van, and they threw them into the back. There were five other men and women in the back of the van.

Onalee was scared and confused. Her heart was racing as the van drove away. During the ride, she and David conversed with the others. They discovered that the other people were all from the East. They wondered why David had been thrown in the van since he was from the West.

When the van stopped thirty minutes later, they were led into a large, well-maintained facility with comfortable chairs and beds. Each person had a room, but they could only talk to one another during meals.

David and Onalee discovered that the people who captured them were not the police. They were civilian authorities—Western civilians who had formed their own group to protect Westerners from people from the East. David was the only hostage to be released. His father had hired a private investigator to find David and his car, which was how the Western civilian group found them. The investigator tracked them down via David's cell phone. After David was set free, his father took him back to Missouri.

David's father was furious, but David was worried about Onalee. He spent hours convincing his dad that Onalee was his best friend and begged him to help her. David's father, realizing how important Onalee was to his son, talked to the private investigator and worked out a possible way for Onalee to be set free and sent back to the East.

Two days later, Onalee was taken into an office for questioning

Robert was in charge of the place. "You'll be going home shortly. We're currently in negotiations with the East, and we're about to make an exchange deal. You'll return to the East, and a citizen from the West will return here."

Several days later, Onalee was driven to the train station and traveled back to the East. Onalee's mother was at the Eastern train station. They greeted one another with joy after Onalee stepped off the train. Her mother drove Onalee back home. Onalee retreated to her bedroom and reflected on her trip. She had no regrets. She was proud of herself for having the strength and will to set out on her journey to the West. She was finally home. It was where she belonged.

CHAPTER 8

Within two weeks, the wall was completed. The chaos within the country ended, but the nation was divided. There was no ending in sight. Families were no longer in conflict because they had no way to communicate or visit relatives from the opposite side.

Tensions arose between politicians from both regions. The president enforced a ban on all travel to and from other countries. People remained in the West, and others remained in the East. That was how American lives were lived.

Most people adjusted to their new lifestyles over time. The killings ceased after the wall divided the two sides. Federal officials made certain that everyone remained on the correct side.

Onalee and David would never meet again—but one dream was fulfilled in the midst of it all.

PART II

PART II

CHAPTER 1

I sat in my room in my hospital gown and stared at the barren white wall.

Dr. Rodriguez knocked on the door and walked in. "How are you feeling today, Savannah?"

"Like I'd like to go home."

"You'll be going home soon, but I want to keep you here for a few more days."

"I finished writing my book," I said.

Dr. Rodriguez checked on me every day during my three-month stay at Mercy Mental Hospital. I was told later on that when I had first arrived, it was as if I was frozen. Apparently, I just stared off into oblivion. I was dazed and confused, but I had no recollection of that. We got along well. Dr. Rodriguez wasn't a typical psychiatrist. He talked a lot—sometimes even small things about his own life.

"Congratulations," said Dr. Rodriguez.

"Thank you," I said.

I told Dr. Rodriguez that I was going to be an author. That led to a brief discussion about dreams and goals. He shared his dream of becoming a professional golfer. He didn't get much time to practice golfing since his priorities were work and family. Before he left, he asked if it would be okay to read my story.

I said, "You'll have to get in line to buy it after it reaches the *New York Times* bestsellers list." I handed him my story, smiled, and said, "Enjoy."

After my brief visit with Dr. Rodriguez, I began my daily routine. I walked down the hallway to the nurses' station to get my morning medication. "I'd like to take a shower today," I said after I took my pills.

"We'll have a nurse get you sometime today for that. In the meantime, don't forget there's a group therapy meeting this morning at eleven," the nurse said.

I thanked her and told her that I would be at the meeting.

My hair was a light shade of brown, but it hadn't been washed in five days. I didn't see the need to take a shower every day while I was in a mental hospital. I mean, there was no one there that I needed to impress. I had spent the past five days engrossed in writing. That day was different. My young children were coming to visit me at four o'clock—and I was certain that my husband was going to be visiting me too.

I retreated to my room after breakfast and waited patiently for a nurse to arrive. It was mandatory that all patients be supervised during showers. A nurse sat outside the shower area because, apparently, some of the patients were threats to themselves. I was merely in the hospital for being anorexic.

By ten thirty, no one had shown up. I got dressed since I never knew when a nurse would arrive. An announcement over the loudspeaker told us that the meeting was about to begin. I walked to the meeting room.

Nurse Patricia started out by saying that it would be Tom's last day at the hospital. He was a well-behaved patient who had only been there a week. During my three-month stay, I had seen patients come and go. There were only two others who had been in as long me. Neither one was someone I really wanted to get to know. Chester rocked back and forth on his seat all day, shouting out different colors. And, Miguel was extremely introverted. I tried to be kind to all of the patients, but when I said anything to Miguel, he hauntingly peered into my eyes and told me to leave him alone. Although they were somewhat depressed, I got along with Sarah and Frank best. I usually sat with them during meals and sometimes played board games with them.

The nurse recited a positive quote and asked us to discuss something positive about the day. When she asked me to begin, I said that my children and husband were visiting that day. "I haven't seen my son Jason or my daughter Amy in a week, and I miss my husband. I can't wait."

"You mean the husband you cheated on?" said Hannah.

My emotions were numb. Her question did not even strike a chord with me. In a previous group, I had shared my immense love for Miles. He was a friend of my sister who I had only known for a brief time. Before I was committed to Mercy Mental Hospital, I fell head over heels in love with him. I had no intention of pursuing any type of relationship with Miles. After all, he was a married man—and I was a married woman. I responded to Hannah's question by simply saying that I never cheated.

"Shawn and I are happily married," I said, "and we are raising two wonderful children. I can't wait to see them."

Chad was sitting next to me, and it was his turn to speak. There were ten patients in the group that day, and I had to listen as they shared the intense issues they were dealing with. A few had even tried to commit suicide.

After the meeting, I ate lunch and waited in my room for a nurse. When she did, I had just enough time to shower and get dressed before my visitors arrived. I wanted to look as good as I possibly could for Shawn. There had been some turbulence in our marriage, especially after I told him I had fallen in love with another man, but I was over that. I was ready to rebuild our marriage. I heard the announcement that visiting hours had begun as I waited patiently in my room.

Ten minutes later, I heard my children in the hallway. I saw my family walking toward me, but there was no Shawn. Jason and Amy had the biggest smiles on their faces when they saw me. I smiled back at them. I looked at the rest of the family and asked where Shawn was. My brother, Ben, told me that he wasn't coming. Still feeling numb, I asked no more questions. I was afraid of the answers.

I didn't enjoy the visit with my family because I was consumed by thoughts of Shawn's absence.

My mother asked what I'd been up to.

I responded, "The usual," forgetting that I had even finished my book. I told her that I was being released soon, and she said that it was good news. I was fragile and vulnerable.

Three days later—after my release from the hospital—I found out that my mother was afraid to tell me that I would not be going back to live with Shawn and my children. My father and mother invited me to live with them, and I did so reluctantly.

CHAPTER 2

Before I was released, Dr. Rodriguez asked to see me in his office. "I read your book," he said. "It was interesting and intriguing,"

"I wrote it metaphorically," I said.

He asked me to elaborate.

"Well, you see, my heart is the United States. The East is one side of my heart, and the West is the other side. It is broken down the middle. The wall represents my broken heart during the war within myself. My heart plays a game of tug-of-war between Miles and Shawn. I don't think my husband wants me anymore, Dr. Rodriguez."

Dr. Rodriguez spent the next thirty minutes with me. He said that being informed about my condition was the first step in the healing process. He stated that my eating habits had improved. He was happy with my weight gain, but I would need therapy twice a month after I left the hospital. Since I hadn't eaten much and lost weight rapidly before I was committed, it severely affected my brain. He explained that my feelings of immense love for Miles were actually intense adrenaline rushes due to self-starvation.

"My marriage may be over, Dr. Rodriguez," I said.

"How do you feel?"

"Numb."

"The East, the West—your book—the wall—it's okay to cry, Savannah," he said.

I looked at him and burst in tears.

He handed me a box of tissues. "You've been holding that in for an extremely long time."

I suppose I had.

A day later, I was released from the hospital and moved in with my parents. Shawn and I eventually divorced. I was allowed visitations with my children. By the time my children were adults, the wall within myself had crumbled. I never published *Mirrors of Me*.

MYSTERY OF THE WINTER FLOWER

A flower bloomed in the winter snow.
From the icy ground below,
Snow fell like crystals.
In the nighttime air,
Heard from a distance were the missiles.
War was an ugly haunting nightmare.
Children grew up very fast,
Trained to fight someday.
Victims of the fiery past,
Their world so dark and gray.
Upon my observation,
A child crying with her friends
Made a declaration.
This would not be her end.
More shots in the distance.
The child was me.
Took the path of least resistance.
Tomorrow she would flee.
Dreaming into the night,
Afraid to run
And afraid to fight.
Though admiration for the midnight sun,
The day has started.
Her day to leave
The course uncharted
On New Year's Eve.
About to leave the past behind,
A flower bloomed in the snow.
The snow's reflection caught her eye.
The flower's shadow like a ghost—

Pink and purple and red and white.
The flower bloomed above the snow,
Bringing daylight from the night.

This—her home—the flower grows.
A child with a dreadful past.
The night is New Year's Eve.
Blossomed as a flower unsurpassed,
Her dreams she believed.
A shadow seen alongside the flower
Is the past left be
New Year came upon the hour.
The flower was really me—
A long, long time ago.
A flower bloomed in the winter snow.

SECRET VAMPIRE SOCIETY

"Legend has it that,
In the darkness filled with bats,
Lurk vampires in the night.
You believe they're out of your sight."
"They choose a victim to bite.
Their neck to their delight,
The vampires suck the victim's blood.
Then sometimes drag them through the mud."
"If the victim doesn't die,
The victim will then try
To bite someone's neck through and through—
For they are now vampires too."
"That is how they live forever.
For they are rather clever.
My story is now done.
Off to bed everyone."
Adaline was at her family's campground
With her parents and children around.
She was a single mother
And camping, too, with her brother.
Everyone had been given a turn
To tell scary stories that made some stomachs churn.
By the campfire that night,
While roasting marshmallows to their delight,
Davis—the brother of Adaline—
Said she was out of line.
He said her story of the vampires
Made her appear to be a liar.
Adaline laughed and said,

"Davis, what's wrong with you in the head?

It was a scary story for fun
After our day of fun in the sun."
Davis said, "I don't think the kids should be subjected to
Stories that are untrue."
Adaline laughed again and said
That she was going to bed.
Davis just shook his head
And, too, went off to bed.
Only the fireflies roamed the campsite
While vampires crept in everyone's dreams that night.

SECRET VAMPIRE SOCIETY PART 2
(TEN YEARS LATER)

"Good-bye," Adaline said with a tear in her eye.
She went inside her home to cry.
Her youngest kid moved out that day,
All of them now grown and living away.
As Adaline cried, she gasped for air.
She had put off her own health care
To devote herself to raising her children
And never even dated men.
She knew something wasn't right.
Her own health care she would no longer fight
And called the doctor the next day.
That her health was okay she prayed.
There had been an appointment cancellation
So, that day, the doctor did an examination.
He was a bit concerned
And told her in two weeks to return.
For she was to have a blood test
Which made her feel a little stressed.
But she had the blood drawn,
Though was afraid her blood would then be all gone.
The following week, the doctor
Called her and shocked her.
He gave her the news that her thyroid was functioning too high.
Everything else was okay though (sigh).
Since the thyroid is in the neck location,
He scheduled her to see the best ENT in the nation.
He said, "Ears, nose, throat doctor is an ENT."
Adaline said, "Oh, I see."
Later, she went to her ENT appointment,

But felt great disappointment
When Graves' disease he diagnosed her with.
He told her it's true and not a myth.

Just before giving Adaline his diagnosis,
He examined her neck and gave his prognosis.
Her levels were too high,
Which made Adaline cry.
The levels mean
The thyroid is functioning too high (she screamed).
Both doctors told her there is no cure—
And that monthly blood work she needed for sure.

SECRET VAMPIRE SOCIETY PART 3

Adaline was unstoppable.
She wasn't going to view her condition as an obstacle.
Rather, she was self-responsible
And met with another doctor at the hospital.
Dr. Barry Costello's office was there.
He was an endocrinologist who cared.
He worked with another doctor named Floyd.
Both were experts treating the thyroid.
Adaline was told that Dr. Costello's schedule was tight,
So she could only get an appointment at night.
"Call me Barry," Dr. Costello said to Adaline.
Adaline replied, "Okay, fine."
Barry said, "I see you've been diagnosed with Graves' disease.
I studied your blood work, and I would agree.
Every week you'll need a blood test."
This was what Barry professed.
Adaline thought every week was too often—
She'd lose all her blood and end up in a coffin—
But she complied
And did abide.
Barry, Dr. Alexander, and Dr. Thomas were now all her doctors.
They took good care of her.
Every week, a needle went into her arm.
Although it pinched, she felt she was in no harm.
Barry was the endocrinologist, you see.
Dr. Alexander—the ENT.
And Dr. Thomas—her general physician.
They all treated her condition.
Gladly they treated her condition
Because they were on a mission.
All three doctors belonged to
A secret vampire society crew.

SECRET VAMPIRE SOCIETY PART 4

"Everyone please sit down."
The vampires' meeting was in a small run-down town.
The vampires and their colleagues were all there.
The new vampires sat in special chairs.
"Tonight is an important meeting.
Tonight we will be greeting
All of the new vampires here—
And handing out an award for vampire of the year."
That is how the meeting began,
After entertainment from their band.
Joshua was the vampire president.
Everyone present was the city's resident.
The city in which they resided within
The vampires blended in.
They worked all different trades
Of which they had done for decades.
They were vampires of the modern day,
Though there were rules that they obeyed.
The modern-day vampires were quite clever,
And this is how they lived forever.
Instead of biting someone's neck,
They would just write out a check.
And to the vampire doctors they would pay
For providing them blood every Wednesday.
How then do you
Become a vampire too?
First your neck
Must be checked
To make sure
You were never bitten years before.

Then you find a victim who
Has Graves' disease too.
They must also have blood type O.

So they can give blood that flows.
For people with O blood types
Can give blood, though, sometimes gripe.
After the victim's blood is drawn,
It is transferred on—
Onto a laboratory the vampires operate
And their colleagues who cooperate.
The modern-day vampires I speak of
Do this all with love.
A victim is never killed—ever.
Though the victim will then, too, live forever.

SECRET VAMPIRE SOCIETY PART 5

The meeting continued on.
Next, Dr. Costello went to the podium.
He had an important announcement,
"I will soon be in retirement."
He said Dr. Alexander and Dr. Thomas would be too.
They had discovered something new—
An antibody in the blood of Adaline
That would make them rich and drinking wine.
"We have discovered a woman—I am no liar
Who has the criteria to be a vampire.
She has the right blood and disease
But something else—you will see."
Joshua raised his hand.
"That sounds quite grand
But what is so special about this girl—
That is better than others in the world?"
Dr. Costello continued on
That his finding he stumbled upon.
You only need one drop of
Her blood—that's enough.
You no longer need to write weekly checks
Or examine anyone's neck.
Just one drop of her blood ever
Will make it so you live forever.
Joshua then asked about the girl:
"Where is she in the world?"
Dr. Costello then realized that, to them,
Adaline was a rare gem.
Suddenly, the meeting adjourned.

Dr. Costello became concerned.
He feared Adaline would be taken away.
He thought he should never have spoken of Adaline that way.

Adaline was truly a gem
To the vampires—all of them.
But Joshua got to her before anyone else.
He told Adaline to say farewell.
"Say farewell to your family and friends—
For you will never see them again.
I am holding you hostage for ransom."
By the way, Joshua was very handsome.
Adaline started to cry—
For she did not understand why.
Joshua was very nice to her though.
He explained everything to her so she would know.
They lived together on the run.
Mostly they had much fun.
A few years passed by—
No one found them except for a spy.

SECRET VAMPIRE SOCIETY PART 6

Adaline was, thus, a hostage
Of the vampires she had knowledge.
Her ransom was never paid.
For someone to pay—she prayed.
Her prayer came somewhat true
For their whereabouts somebody knew.
The person's name was Romero.
He would become Adaline's hero.
Joshua and Adaline would soon be fleeting
For Romero had been at the vampire meeting.
He was a vampire too—
The nicest one anyone knew.
He was searching always for Adaline
And found the two of them in time.
They had been staying at a cabin in the woods,
Eating soup and canned goods.
Adaline's health was failing—
She was ailing.
For she was taken from there—
From the doctors who cared.
Just then, Romero knocked in the door.
He punched Joshua to the floor
Then grabbed Adaline's hand
And both of them ran.
"Get into my car.
We have to travel far."
Adaline did as told.
Romero had a heart of gold.
And so the story goes.

To Adaline, Romero proposed.
Both were vampires forever
And also very clever.

For they offered for free
To anybody
A drop of blood from Adaline.
The world stood in a long line.
Eventually, everybody became a vampire too—
And the world grew.
Because no one ever died.
If they did, they lied.
So to cure world population,
There were good-bye celebrations.
Vampires traveled to planets other than Earth
Where to baby vampires they gave birth.
Thus, Earth and many planets in the solar system
No longer had victims.
Each person was to live forever with laughter—
Happily ever after.

    If reading this story was a pain in the neck
        And you think this story sucks,
            Remember …
          It's a vampire story!

THE PROMISE—
(FIRST COUPLE)

INTRODUCTION

A promise was made by a couple in love, but their commitment to one another faded over time. They said they would stay true to each other while they were apart. Although, when they parted from each other, they both found someone else. The promise? It was to always be there.

(SECOND COUPLE)

CHAPTER 1

The Campfire

It's Halloween night. A boy and a girl are roasting marshmallows and eating pizza around a campfire.

"Tell me a story—one of your wondrous stories," he says.

The girl decided to keep it interesting and not boring. "The story is a true story. It is called 'The Ghost in You.' Do you believe in magic?"

The boy shook his head and said, "No, I don't believe in magic."

The girl exclaimed, "My story is set in 1978." She began to build a mystery.

(THIRD COUPLE)

CHAPTER 2

The Haunted House

The house I was inside of was haunted. It was old and run down. There were spiderwebs in every corner. Zombie backstabbers were following the boy I was with—and they were following me. As they approached us, we heard them chanting that they were going to kill us. We wondered how we were going to save our lives.

The boy insisted he knew the right way out of there. "Follow me," he said with sheer confidence. We walked through long, unlit hallways. Our flashlights were all we had.

As we passed by several doors, the boy opened them a crack, peered inside using his flashlight, and continued on. I followed close behind. He was leading me in mysterious ways through a crazy maze.

Our flashlights lit up a door at the end of the hallway. He opened it, and we saw an old, worn cement staircase. He took my hand and led me down into a basement. Another door was there. He opened that one too. It was somewhat large and looked intriguing.

We stepped inside, and the door quickly shut behind us. We were startled. I turned around to open the door, but it was locked. We were trapped. It was a good thing that it was dark so he couldn't see my anger. My emotions settled down after a while. I wanted to venture out of the room, but he wanted to sit and stew. I decided to explore and find a way out on my own.

CHAPTER 3

The Great Escape

I found another staircase. It was the same as the other one. It was old and made of cement. I thought it would lead me to an exit. When I reached the top of the staircase, sure enough, it led me to an old wooden porch that made creaking sounds with each step I took.

I enjoyed breathing the fresh air and felt a sense of relief that I was out of there. Not wanting to stay any longer, I quickly stepped down from the porch and began a journey by myself.

I walked for a couple of miles in the dense fog. There was nothing but a sign that said "Point of No Return." The road was in the middle of fields of long, tall weeds.

Suddenly, out of nowhere, an invisible man appeared. I could only see his clothing. He was the only person I had encountered since I left the haunted house. I felt relieved to have found someone. I told him I was lost.

He said nothing.

I asked for directions away from this place.

He pointed down the road and handed me daisies.

I thanked him and continued down the road.

CHAPTER 4

The Train

It only took a short time before I saw a sign for Gray Street. It was nice to know where I was. I was unfamiliar with the area, but I saw streetlights in the distance. I approached the lights and saw about twenty of them, but only two were lighting up an old train station.

There was an entrance to the station, but I was afraid to go inside. It appeared to be dark and gloomy inside. I felt worn out from all the walking I had done. I stood near the tracks, wondering what to do next.

I heard a train approaching the station, and a bright headlight pierced my eyes. It stopped right at the station. No one got off the train, but the passenger car door opened. I thought I had two choices—to stay or get on the train—and I chose the latter.

"All aboard. Calling all ghosts. Boarding time to all ghosts," the conductor shouted.

The train was also known as the ghost train. There were thirteen ghosts on the train, including the conductor. Each ghost had a partner. The partners were typically ghosts that they had never met before. Every ghost looked human, but they all had white skin and white hair (not Caucasian—literally white). The conductor, however, looked like a living human being. I don't think he was a ghost.

I boarded the train. The conductor read a statement to me: "Welcome. May I first say congratulations on making your entrance onto the train, which leads to heaven? It is an honor to have you here. I sincerely hope you enjoy your stay."

I knew there had been a misunderstanding. "I'm alive!" I repeated over and over.

The conductor told me there was not a mistake. "It is a foolproof system," he said. He asked for my ticket, but the only thing I had were the daisies from the invisible man.

I handed the conductor a daisy.

He took off each petal and told me to take a seat. "Take a seat. Aisle 3. Your partner is Lenny. Enjoy your trip."

I took my seat and introduced myself to Lenny. He seemed friendly. Lenny was white and had white hair. He wore glasses, a plaid flannel shirt, and old jeans. His earbuds were attached to a television. Each seat on the train had a small television.

I took a good look around the train. An eerie feeling overtook my body. Everyone looked like ghosts. *What if I am dead? What if I look like a ghost?* I needed to find a mirror to make sure I still looked the same. The only items in my possession were the daisies from the invisible man.

The other passengers were communicating with each other just as live humans would. I thought I would ask the passengers if they had a mirror. I turned to the ghost behind my seat and introduced myself. I noticed he was wearing a name tag. In fact, everyone on board had a name tag except me. His name was Carlos. "No, I don't have a mirror," he replied. His partner must have overheard me. Her name tag said, "Adrielle." Adrielle was wearing fashionable jeans, sneakers, and a sweatshirt. She looked to be a teenager. Adrielle reached into her backpack and pulled out a mirror. "Here," she said.

I replied, "Thank you." I took the mirror from Adrielle and gazed into it. I was not a bit surprised. I looked the same as I always had. "Adrielle, does everyone on this train look like a ghost to you?"

Adrielle replied, "Yes, everyone but you."

It was just as I thought. I was different than the others. *I must be alive. But why am I here? Why am I on a train with ghosts?*

Lenny tapped me on the shoulder. "You should sit down."

Lenny and I tried to watch my television, but the train stopped moving and the televisions went dead. Everyone remained calm except for me. "Where are we?" I shouted.

The conductor walked down the aisle and said that there was a temporary delay. "In the meantime, we can get to know each other. Let's start by saying our first name and one thing about ourselves."

I felt like I was back in school. I thought that the conductor would choose me to begin since I stood out, but he pointed to Lenny and asked to begin.

"I'm Lenny, and one thing about me is that I was a computer technician."

"Carlos is my name, and I was married with five children."

"My name is Adrielle, and I played soccer in school."

Giovanni owned a restaurant. Hedy was a widow and hoped to see her husband again. KC was a florist, Rupert was a painter, Maurice owned a casino, Skye was an actress, Nala loved animals, and Ace was a race-car driver. I thought it would be my turn next, but the conductor left—and the train began moving.

CHAPTER 5

Elevator
(Ground Level—Reservations)

The train abruptly stopped. Everyone was getting off the train and entering the train station. I decided to follow. Outside the run-down station, there was a golden sign for "Heaven's Station." The inside was like a beautiful elegant hotel.

Above the reservation desk, a big streamer said, "Congratulations." I suppose it was there because we had made it to the entrance to heaven. Lenny was still by my side. All the ghosts formed a line at the counter, but Lenny and I wanted to ask the concierge some questions.

The concierge was dressed in a business suit. Lenny asked about this place, and she told us all about it. She said that floors one through six were for training and to find out who we were to help, floor seven was heaven, and the floors beyond seven were for all the concerts and parties in heaven. Lenny and I were intrigued. Our eyes lit up as soon as she mentioned concerts and parties.

"Thank you for the information," Lenny said.

We headed over toward the reservations desk and noticed that the ghosts had already checked in. They were all headed toward the elevators for training before entering heaven.

Lenny turned toward me and whispered, "How'd you like to check out some concerts and parties with me?" The offer sounded tempting. I hesitated, but then I said I would like to venture with him.

I walked to the elevator with Lenny. There were endless floor buttons on the elevator. We waited for the ghosts to leave and pressed floor eight. The ride was long enough to hear one of my favorite songs.

CHAPTER 6

Elevator
(Floor 8—Concert)

Lenny and I stepped off the elevator on the eighth floor. It looked like we were outdoors. The sky was endless, and people were everywhere. I heard a lot of music. Bands were performing on many stages. It was just as I would imagine it was at Woodstock—but endless.

Lenny nudged me and wanted me to follow him through the crowd. As we managed our way, the crowd parted for us. I thought we must be special. They were making a way for us to get to our destination. I wasn't quite sure where Lenny was leading me.

It soon became apparent where Lenny was headed. "My favorite band when I was a kid," he said. "They died in a plane crash." I had never heard the band before, but they sounded amazing. We listened to the band for a while, but I still felt eyes peering at us. Whenever I looked around, people were gazing at us. I realized that everyone else had wings.

Oh no. I don't even look like a ghost! At least Lenny has that going for him.

Suddenly, all the music stopped. An announcer approached a microphone and stated that there was a brief intermission. He said that the main attraction would be next. I wondered who it would be.

I saw people with wings going to concession stands during the intermission. Lenny and I didn't want to lose our front-row spot, and we remained there. The announcer checked the microphone and said, "It gives me great pleasure to announce the most amazing superstar heaven has ever had the privilege to have play on the eighth floor. Please welcome this superstar to today's production."

I looked around as everyone's wings fluttered and people clapped. All of a sudden, one of my favorite singers walked out onto the stage. I couldn't believe my eyes! He had died of heart problems. Suddenly, he began his performance. He sang all the songs I knew. His dance moves left everyone dazed.

The announcer walked up to the microphone with a note. "A message has been sent here from the seventh floor. It reads, 'The two who broke into the eighth floor, and you know who you are, please remove yourselves. An old saying goes like this: work before pleasure. Report to the first floor immediately for instructions to your destination. Signed with love, The Big Boss.' Would the two who this is addressed to please follow the orders and head to the elevators now?"

Lenny and I looked at one another. We knew it was meant for us. We walked toward the elevators, and the crowd parted for us. I realized that it did not mean we were special. It meant we weren't angels yet.

On our way down to the first floor, Lenny started calling me "Angel."

I said, "That's not my name."

Lenny said, "It's my nickname for you."

I thought it was sweet.

We reached the first floor and stepped off the elevator.

A ghostly woman was waiting for us. "I'm here to give you instructions to your destination."

I was afraid we were going to hell for disobeying the rules.

"Take a seat over there." She pointed to comfortable seats in the lobby.

We headed to the waiting room and sat down.

The ghostly woman went in the opposite direction.

"La de da da da do da," I said as we waited.

An hour later, she returned. "You are to report to the second floor."

"Is that it?" I asked.

She gave me a nasty look and followed us onto the elevators. She pressed the button for the second floor. As Lenny and I stepped out of the elevator, the ghostly woman followed. I later discovered that she would be our teacher on the second floor.

CHAPTER 7

Elevator
(Floor 2—Training—Forgiveness 101)

It was my first day of class. I felt out of place. Yes, I am Caucasian, but I am not as white as these ghosts were. The class was Forgiveness 101, and the teacher was Miss Griver—the ghostly woman who put us in time-out in the waiting room. Miss Griver began the class with a poem. It read like this:

FORGIVENESS

Lord knows I tried
With all of my might
To make things right.
Just after our fight,
I refused to bend
When you tried to mend.
Even when down on your knee,
I just couldn't see.
A simple fight
To shed some light
Arguing into the night
To see who's right.
Did it all matter?
The dish that was shattered,
The pieces scattered,
Good hearts battered.
Don't hold a grudge

>Because of your ego
>And need to show
>That better you know.
>Because one day we'll die.
>And our chance will pass by.
>But I broke the tie.
>So this is good-bye.
>It's not just a quote—
>I learned what they wrote.
>So I bought a sailboat
>And quoted the quote.
>This is the quote on my boat—
>No joke:
>"Life is short" and not long.
>Please believe when I say
>I learned I was wrong
>After so long.
>I called the next day.
>When down at the bay,
>They said you passed away—
>And that I missed you by one day.

"That, class, is a poem written by the famous Carolyn Croop. Can anyone tell me what this poem means?" asked Miss Griver.

I raised my hand, but Miss Griver pointed to KC and let her explain the meaning.

KC summed up the poem by saying that life is short—so forgive those you love.

"Very good," Miss Griver said.

Miss Griver then gave the class an assignment. We were to write our own poems about forgiveness. She gave us thirty minutes to complete it. Mine was this:

PART-TIME GHOST

>I walked out my door
>To the outside.
>No one said hi anymore.

Inside, I cried.
I'm alive!
I'm in the world!
I went for a drive.
I was unfurled.
I arrived at my destination—
A party for my son.
For my family is my salvation.
Every time I think I'm done,
They spoke to me.
I knew I was loved
And me they could see.
Their time I was worthy of.
The rest of the world, however,
Didn't seem to notice me.
So I tried to be clever
Then me they would see.
I went to a secondhand shop
And bought a spotlight.
For me you cannot stop.
In the light, I would shine so bright.
I brought it to my home
And stared at it forever.
Where I lived alone,
All ties I had severed
Within the brilliance of my mind.
I could not understand.
Would I ever find
A place for me to land?
Somewhere I was not a ghost
By myself and scorned.

My observation post
Became the world that mourned.
The spotlight then shined brighter
On my face that day.
I turned into a writer
And this is what I had to say:
I'm sorry to my friends

The ones from the past.
I put an end
To friendships that should last.
The bridges that I burned
Were merely a way to cope
With my own concerns.
Of my world with little hope,
I'm the one who lost.
Friends worth knowing,
I paid the cost.
My ghost side I am now showing.
I then walked out my door again.
The world was just the same—
Nothing written with my pen
Brought me to my fame.
I found a mirror
And stared at myself.
It became clear.
I had become but a memory on a shelf.
No one knew me,
But only a few.
Was I too late to be
A friend like new?
I left the graveyard
And drove off into the sunset,
Following a star
Leaving behind all regrets.

 Miss Griver read my poem and told me I passed the class. "We must forgive," Miss Griver said. "It brings a sense of peace to all. It brings closure to certain situations. To earn your wings in heaven, you must learn to forgive."

 When we heard the ringing of a bell, I thought, *An angel got its wings.*

 Everyone started filing out of the classroom, and I realized that class was over.

 Miss Griver shouted, "Forgiveness goes both ways."

CHAPTER 8

Elevator
(Floor 3—Training—Friendliness 101)

I looked around the room, but Lenny was nowhere in sight.

The teacher looked down on me and said, "You're getting a second chance."

I was dumbfounded. "I don't understand," I said.

"I understand that you and Lenny entered into floors beyond heaven. You were told not to go any farther than the seventh floor until you earned your wings."

I was in Friendliness Training 101. My teacher was Mrs. Kindly.

"Thank you for the second chance," I said.

Mrs. Kindly replied, "You're welcome. Friendliness is a key component in life as exemplified by a poem by Carolyn Croop."

PEACE, HARMONY, AND THE HUMAN RACE

To help us organize,
We categorize.
We need to accept
But not disrespect.
None of us are the same,
And life is not a game.
Our differences make us who we are.
Each individual—a shining star.
Today I got a notion
To research all the human emotions.
There are approximately seventy-two.
I will list them to review:

Affection, anger, angst, anguish, annoyance, anxiety, arousal, awe, boredom, confidence, contempt, contentment, courage, disgust, distrust, dread, ecstasy, embarrassment, envy, euphoria, excitement, fear, frustration, gratitude, grief, guilt, happiness, hatred, hope, horror, hostility, hurt, hysteria, indifference, interest, jealousy, joy, loathing, loneliness, love, lust, outrage, panic, passion, pity, pleasure, pride, rage, regret, relief, remorse, sadness, satisfaction, self-confidence, shame, shock, shyness, sorrow, suffering, surprise, terror, trust wonder, worry, zeal, and zest.

> Just think, if you will,
> To develop a skill
> To be congenial to others
> To live in harmony with one another.
> Because the same human emotion
> (I say this with much devotion)
> Is many times a different one than
> People you're with or in your clan.
> Here is my magical potion.
> Take the list of human emotions.
> Focus on the positive ones.
> It will help you in the long run.
> Count your blessings each and every day.
> That will, too, help along the way
> Feelings and emotions are never wrong.
> Negative ones—accept then move along.
> Yes, I am trying to teach,
> And this is what I preach.
> Every person's life is like a song.
> Let's sing in harmony and get along.

"Now class," the teacher said, "Do you completely understand? Be kind to one another."

The bell rang, and we were all told to go to the next level. Even though it was the school bell, I wondered if an angel was getting its wings. I headed to the elevator for my next class.

CHAPTER 9

Elevator
(Floor 4—Training—Music 101)

I was wondering if I was going to learn how to play the harp in music class. Later, I was told that the harp is taught only to those who earn their wings. That would occur on floor nine. The class was Music 101, and the teacher's name was Mrs. Harper.

Mrs. Harper handed me a flute. "It's a magical flute," she said.

I didn't know there was magic in heaven. I thought it was like voodoo and unholy. "Magic in heaven?" I asked.

"Magic is everywhere dear," she replied. Mrs. Harper taught me how to summon the angels. I played the tune, and four angels entered the room. Nora, Olivia, Elliott, and Leon all had wings.

Nora asked if the class needed help.

Mrs. Harper explained that she was demonstrating a class lesson, thanked them for showing up, and told them they could leave. "Anytime you're in need of help, remember the magic of music. Music is like a healing stone. It soothes, it teaches, and it does innumerable things. It is the universal language."

CHAPTER 10

Elevator
(Floor 5—Training—Giving 101)

The next class was Giving 101. Professor Wright began class by reading a poem.
I raised my hand.
The professor pointed to me and said, "What is your question, ma'am?"
I joked and said, "I'm assuming the poem is by Carolyn Croop?"
Professor Wright did not find me to be funny and began reading the poem.

LETTER

Dear loved one,
How do you do?
I gave to you.
You took.
I gave to others too.
Give me a second look.
I am not who you think I am.
For you surprised me by what you said.
I now say, "Damn."
Your words ricochet in my head.
You had thought that taking from me
Would backfire on you.
Please understand and see
When I give to you and others too—
I was never looking for repayment
That is part of who I am.

> I thought you knew me better—
> No schemes or scams.
> So I write this letter.
> I give and give—
> Sometimes I even wonder why.
> I get nothing in return to live.
> Though it does not make me cry,
> I rarely ever think that though
> And give because I care.
> Even if it does not show,
> I give to you and share.
> Thank you when you gave to me.
> Though I do not keep score,
> I believe God is in his glee
> With laughter like a roar.
> For he knows me quite well—
> As I thought you did too.
> No ill intentions to tell.
> Look at me from a different view.
> I am now ending this letter.
> I look out for those in need.
> I'm hoping now you know me better.
> For those I love—I bleed.
> Sincerely,
> Me
> P.S. I love you dearly—
> My giving is free.

"And that is the end of the poem," said Professor Wright. "Any thoughts from anyone?"

Hedy raised her hand, and I was surprised because Hedy rarely talked. "Professor Wright, sir, when can I see my husband? He gave me joy and happiness in life. We were married for fifty-one years before he passed away. Please, sir, I just want to see him again."

Professor Wright did not give Hedy the answer. Instead, he said that she was on the right path. I figured that must mean I was on the right path too.

The bell rang, and we all went to the next class.

CHAPTER 11

Elevator
(Floor 6—Training—Love 101)

I was ready for my last training class before entering heaven. The teacher was Mr. Robinson, and the topic was love. I was hesitant about the class since I had never been very lucky in love.

The class settled in, and I raised my hand.

Mr. Robinson hadn't even had a chance to speak, but he pointed at me and asked, "Yes?"

"Since we're close to graduating and entering heaven, I was wondering what happens if we end up failing?"

Mr. Robinson looked mad. He said, "No one has ever failed their entrance into heaven. No one."

I felt a sense of relief, but I doubted if I would ask any more questions.

Mr. Robinson stated, "To begin, I will be reading a poem by Carolyn Croop. This poem shows that love hurts and love can be lost. It also shows that the heart can begin to heal."

FLATLINED LOVE

Love
Lost
Cold
Frost
Heart
Spark
Rain

Pain
Now
Numb
You were the only one,
But my waiting is done.
I feel no more
And never will.
Love
Lost
Cold
Frost
Heart
Spark
Rain
Pain
Now
Numb
Flatlined love

Mr. Robinson shared one more poem by Carolyn Croop. It is to be read from left to right for a story and top to bottom for words relating to love or romance. He handed out the poem and read from left to right.

THIS GOLD RING

It began with a	date
When we	swa
yed as we danced	in
an embrace which I	lo
nged fore	ver
I	followe
d his lead as he whispe	r
ed, you're	beau
tiful, charming, luscious, and	sweet
Then	he
gave me a shrewd,	art

ful good-bye and	par
ted. In	a mo
ment's time the reason was clea	r
	A to
tal stranger, another	wo
man had been there to win him	o
v	er
Yet	young
love always f	i
nds its way back from	dol
lar to something that's	true
That which is	love
We don't have the	gall
to remember our bad	ant
iquities	fi
nding rom	ance
is enough in	love
So in	cas
e	an ova
l-shaped ring should appear	A
loud I pray I will someday say I	do, re
membering that great dance	r
who wears his white	suit, or
the dream of our	honey
moon to	Rome, o
r some	romantic
place, or believing in that moment when	H
e and I became	us
with this, his wedding	band

    Class was over. We were to get back on the elevator and go to the seventh floor for graduation.
    I felt a tap on my shoulder.
    Mr. Robinson handed me a folded card.

I opened it and read the word: "Fail." I looked at Mr. Robinson and his evil eyes.

He said, "This is an embarrassment. You are the only ghost to have ever failed in love. This does not look good on me or heaven's reputation." Mr. Robinson explained that when ghosts fail a class, they must go back to the ground level, board the ghost train again, and be assigned one person to help in the living world. "Go back to where you came from. Immediately!"

I never made it to the gates of heaven and graduation. I failed in love. Walking slowly and sadly toward the elevator, I looked back to see that the other ghosts were following close behind me. I thought they must be there to support me.

Adrielle pushed the up button on the elevator as I pressed the down button. As I rode the elevator down by myself, I thought, *I never found out who I was to help.*

CHAPTER 12

Elevator (Ground Level)

I exited the building and hopped back on the ghost train. I thought I would be alone, but a few other ghosts were on the train. I was surprised to see that Lenny was there. I asked why he was back on the train. He said he had failed Forgiveness. A couple of the other ghosts said they failed Friendliness. That made sense to me since I had found them to be rather rude. They said they were taking the train back to their hometowns so that they could haunt people.

"How did you fail Forgiveness, Lenny?" I asked.

He responded that he was never able to forgive his brother for stealing from him. "That teacher up there—Miss Griver—says I need to love him. Not after what he did. Now I have to help him!"

I asked, "Lenny, what did he steal from you?"

"Fifty thousand dollars. I lent Earl the money out of the goodness of my heart. After all, he has three rug rats to feed. He only paid me back twenty dollars at a time. I never got the full amount."

I said, "What do you have to help him with?"

Lenny said, "I just have to make sure he's all right." Lenny began to watch his television.

"What's on television?" I asked.

Lenny looked at me, took out his earbuds, and said, "I'm busy studying. These televisions broadcast the life of the person we are to help. If you fail a class, you're sent down here to help someone in need."

I was curious about who I was to help and turned on my television. The only thing I heard was white noise. For a split second, I saw the flashing of a person. I could almost swear it was me. I turned to Lenny and said,

"Sorry to bother you again. My television isn't working. Do you know what I should do?"

Lenny said, "Not a clue."

The train stopped at various train stations. Ghosts exited and entered the train.

Lenny said it was his turn to exit.

I suddenly felt sad. "I'll miss you," I said.

"Good luck," he said. He was returning to his hometown to make peace with a few people from his life, especially Earl. "They'll come to know me as Lenny the friendly ghost."

I laughed. When he exited the train, I instantly was back to feeling sad.

The train continued on with Nala, Skye, and Maurice. Nala and Skye were partners.

Maurice's partner, Rupert, had graduated into heaven.

"So, ugly ghost thing, what did you fail?" Nala said.

I didn't think her rude remark deserved a response, but I said, "I failed in love."

Laughter erupted throughout the train. "No way!" Skye said. "Really?"

I could feel my face getting red. "Really?"

The laughter got louder. Ghosts talked amongst themselves and peered in my direction.

Trying to remain positive, I said, "But I passed all of the other classes!"

No one seemed to care.

I decided to turn the tables. "So what was it that you all failed?"

Nala responded, "Not your business, ugly face."

I didn't have to question her any farther. I was quite certain she had failed Friendliness Training 101.

Maurice said, "You know, you may be different than the rest of us, but you sure are cute. Must have had the boys chasing you in life. Oh, and I didn't pass music class."

I was stunned. I enjoyed music so much that I couldn't understand anyone ever failing it. "Why?"

"Because I told the teacher she was a cutie. I told her she had one lucky husband."

"And that got you kicked out of school and back on this train?" I asked.

"Well, um, I might have said a few other things."

"I see." I wasn't sure I really wanted to know what he had said to Mrs. Harper. He must have been a womanizer or an obnoxious flirt in life. "What did you fail, Skye?"

Skye replied, "Giving. I guess I spent too much time in life buying material things,—houses, furniture, designer clothes, and other things—that I never really gave to many people. And I still don't think I needed to."

I could see why Skye was back on the train. She needed to learn a lesson on giving. And Maurice needed better manners. Nala needed to be kind. *But I know about love. I mean, I think I do. Why could I never keep a relationship? Why was I alone in life?*

The train stopped, and the ghosts got off.

Lenny boarded the train.

"Lenny!" I shouted.

"Hey," he said.

"I thought I'd never see you again! This is amazing! Why are you here?" I asked.

"I need your help," he replied.

CHAPTER 13

Lenny's Hometown

The train continued down the tracks, and Lenny had a serious look on his face. "It's Earl," he said. "I need your help."

"What's the problem, Lenny?" I asked.

"I can't do it alone, Angel. Earl's homeless—living on the streets with a paper bag around a bottle of booze. He has a wife and three kids at home, struggling to survive without him. He's not a man. He's a drunk—a downright boozed-up drunk. How am I supposed to help someone I have no respect for? How am I supposed to help him being a ghost? Angel, you're the only one of us who looks alive. Come with me and talk some sense into my brother. Please. I don't know any other way."

I paused for a few moments. *Lenny said I look alive. I do look alive. I'm the only who does. He's right. Well, except for the conductor. He looked like a live human being too. But I wasn't sure I knew how to help someone who was homeless and drank too much. In life, I just minded my own business. I did the daily things that needed to be done—and that was it. Oh, God. Could this be who I was to help? Earl? No, it couldn't be. Earl was Lenny's assignment. Maybe I was to help Lenny. No, that couldn't be either. Lenny was a ghost. Who was I to help—and why would no one tell me?*

"Okay, Lenny, I'll give it a shot."

"Thank you. Thank you." Lenny took my hand and led me toward the train's doors.

I jumped back a little as the doors flew open.

Lenny led me out of the train and into his hometown.

We walked for about a mile and saw older homes along our path. I joked with him that it would be quicker if he had earned his wings and could fly.

Wait—ghosts can fly. They can go through walls and haunt people and open and close drawers. "Lenny, why aren't you flying?"

"Well, you see, there's this girl by my side who can't fly. If I were to take flight without her, she'd be lost."

"Okay, I get it," I said as I smiled at him.

At midnight, I could still see streetlights. We walked a little farther, and Lenny pointed to a corner store. "Look."

I wasn't sure what he wanted me to see.

"There he is," Lenny said.

"Where?"

"At the edge of the store ... in front."

I saw a man sitting in the parking lot. As we approached the store, I got a closer look at the man.

"That's Earl," Lenny said. "Go talk some sense into him, Angel."

I paused for a moment. "I'll do my best, Lenny." I had no idea what to say or where to begin. "Hello?"

Earl looked up at me with tired, sad eyes. Those were the eyes of a man who was ashamed of his situation—the eyes of a man who wanted a way out of that situation but didn't know the way. Earl didn't say a word back to me.

I was determined to help Lenny. I hadn't come all this way to fail. "Do you need a blanket or anything?"

Earl closed his eyes and fell asleep.

A store employee came outside to empty the trash cans and shouted, "Scram, old man!"

Earl remained asleep.

The employee went inside and came out a few seconds later with a broom. He used it to nudge Earl and told him to leave. The store employee said nothing to me.

I assumed he thought I was a customer who was observing the scene.

Earl got up with his bottle of booze and began staggering toward the sidewalk.

"Talk to him," Lenny said.

I nodded and walked over to Earl. "Sir, I know you don't know me, but I know you."

Earl didn't look impressed. He continued staggering on his way.

"Does the name Lenny mean anything to you?"

Earl stopped dead in his tracks and looked at me with shock and sadness in his eyes. "Who are you?"

"Just someone who wants to help you. I know, I mean, I knew your brother. Lenny was a good friend of mine. He told me your situation, and I'd like to help you."

Earl began talking to me as though he hadn't had even one drink. We walked down the sidewalk and talked the entire way to his cardboard box in the woods behind some houses.

Lenny was right behind us, but Earl could not see or hear him.

I said good night and let him get some sleep.

"Well?" Lenny said.

"What do you mean?" I asked.

"What's your plan? How are you going to get him away from booze and back to where he belongs—at home with his family?"

"I don't know."

Lenny looked mad and disappointed.

"Lenny, I don't know a lot, but this is what I do know. He's an alcoholic. It's a disease. It is not a character flaw. There's a chemical imbalance inside his brain. The money he took from you—did he use it for alcohol?"

"What do you think? Of course he did."

"He's lost, Lenny. He told me he's a veteran. I read about a veteran who said he'd rather have respect than money. Maybe that's all he needs. Well, respect and professional help. I have an idea. After Earl wakes up, you and I will talk to him. You will tell me what to say."

Lenny said, "He won't want to hear what I have to say."

"Lenny, have you heard nothing I have said? Drop the hardened heart. This may be your last chance to make peace with him—and peace with yourself."

Lenny stared at me for a minute. I could tell he was thinking about what I said.

We spent the night talking. We found a park close to where Earl was sleeping and sat together on a park bench. As the sun rose, people began walking by. Some people were walking their dogs, some were jogging, and some were simply walking through the park. A few people stared strangely at me, but I didn't really understand why. It then occurred to me that they couldn't see Lenny—they could only see me—and I must have appeared to be talking to myself. I wondered why I didn't need any sleep.

Lenny suggested that we go check on Earl and told me what to say to him.

"Earl, wake up. It's time to wake up."

Earl's eyes opened wide, and a smile formed on his face.

"Before he died, Lenny told me that he loves you. He was sad he never made peace with you. He said to not worry about the money you owed him. Don't sleep your life away, Earl. It's time to live."

Our conversation lasted all day. The best part was that he never had any alcohol. At the end of the day, he said he was done with alcohol and was going home to his wife and kids. We said our good-byes, and I began to walk away.

He shouted, "Thank you, Angel."

Lenny led the way back to the ghost train. The doors opened, and I hopped inside. The doors quickly shut. "Stop the train," I shouted.

Lenny didn't make it inside the train. The train stopped, and the doors opened.

"This is your chance," I said. "Get on board."

Lenny said, "I'm going to stay here a little while longer. I want to make sure Earl is all right."

"Is this really good-bye?"

"Yes, Angel. I have only one thing to say to you besides thank you."

Small tears filled my eyes as I waited to hear what Lenny was going to say.

"Catch a concert or two while you can."

The doors shut, and the train continued down the tracks. That was the last time I saw Lenny. *Catch a concert or two while you can? What is the meaning behind that?* I pondered that for a few moments until I realized he meant live a little.

As the days passed, I realized that everyone had exited the train except me and a zombie who was sitting toward the back. He didn't bother me until he got up from his seat and headed toward me. He was armed and extremely dangerous.

As he ran toward me, the train came to an abrupt stop. It was my only chance to escape. The doors opened, and I exited as fast as I could.

Fortunately, the zombie remained on the train.

CHAPTER 14

The Indian Reservation

There was not a train station, but there was a sign for an "Indian Reservation." Falling to my knees, I prayed for salvation. I shouted, "Save me. Save me."

A spirit voice talked back to me, which made me glad that I was not alone. The voice said, "Just breathe. You'll soon be home."

I wondered who was talking to me. I asked, "Spirit voice, tell me your name."

The voice whispered, "The Ghost in You. You've been barely breathing down under. Look for the light."

I was in shock and said, "This is some kind of mistake."

The invisible man reappeared and told me not to be afraid.

I asked where I was and what was happening to me.

The invisible man responded that he was a magician—and this was all a show.

I said, "Why am I here?"

He told me he was giving me everything he owned, including his magic powers.

I told him I didn't need everything he owned. "The only thing I want to know is how to love."

The man waved his wand and said, "Abracadabra—don't look back." He handed me his magic wand and disappeared.

I was still in shock and shouted, "I need you!"

A messenger arrived and handed me a note: "I'll be the light."

(SECOND COUPLE)

CHAPTER 15

Storyteller's Conclusion

"And this concludes my story," the girl said to the boy.

The boy was fast asleep by the campfire.

She noticed that the fire had burned out. She looked over at him, smiled, and went to sleep too.

(FIRST COUPLE)

CHAPTER 16

The Ending

Hello. Yes, it's me. The joker. The master storyteller. The author of this story. Didn't I blow your mind? I write this tale as a way to cope. If I have laughter, then I can get by without you. Even though we have been far apart, you have always been with me in spirit. I'm sorry that this story has no "happily ever after."

Just as I was finished writing this story, my phone lit up. "Boo!" the text said.

I had no idea who this was from. "I miss you," it went onto say. "Meet me for dessert."

It was my Boo. My one real love. I was baffled.

"Remember the promise we made?" the text said. "Wherever you will go, our love will never fade. As long as you love me—got to believe in magic!"

THE THREE-SIDED LADY

I know of a lady
Who has three sides.
She appears rather shady
Because each day she prays then lies.
Her three sides are that she lies
And that she always goes to church.
Somehow she still walks with pride.
The third side I once researched.
I found out she was an actress
Worth about
One billion less some taxes.
Show biz, though, she was kicked out.
So there's the story as it is—
A lady with money who prays and lies.
She knew a man and once was his.
Now she cries behind her disguise.
I wonder about her existence.
Could she be content?
Her lies unceasingly consistent—
Her money shrewdly spent.
I knew of a lady with three sides.
She is known nationwide.
I wonder when she will decide
To step outside of her disguise.
The lady with three sides—
I know her well by just my eyes.

THE WITNESS

CHAPTER 1

The tires screeched as Brooke pulled into the city parking garage on a cold December morning. Brooke put the car in park and let out a sigh. Without much thought, she stepped out of the car and gathered her belongings. Her book bag was filled with two days of clothes and personal care items. Brooke was on her way to a shelter for women who had been abused.

It was about two o'clock in the morning. Brooke had called the shelter to let them know she was on her way. She was escaping the mental, emotional, and physical abuse of her boyfriend.

As Brooke walked down the ramp, she could only hear her own footsteps. A few cars passed by on the street below, but no people were in sight. She knew it was a dangerous location. The city had a reputation for crime. Brooke walked as rapidly as possible without making herself look vulnerable.

The shelter was on the other side of Main Street, which meant that she had to walk through an unlit alley. Brooke approached the alley. The coast looked clear, and she continued through as the streetlights disappeared. Brooke heard male voices, and a shot was fired. The gunman ran out through the alley without noticing Brooke.

Brooke's nerves felt like they were about to burst. Though doing her best to stay calm, she decided to continue to the end of the alley. If she turned back, there would be nowhere for her to find a safe haven away from Raymond. The shelter was so close, and she made the choice to go forward.

Three men ran from the scene. She caught a glimpse of their clothing. All three were dressed in dark hoodies and dark pants. One of the men made eye contact with her for a second. A few steps later, she witnessed the blood on the ground.

Picking up her speed, Brooke entered the shelter.

A weary security guard sat inside the entrance.

Brooke thought that the security guard must see this sort of thing all the time. She looked at the guard and said, "I just witnessed a shooting."

The guard sat up, questioned her a bit, and called the police.

Within four minutes, the police were questioning her. Sergeant Hannigan stepped away to take a phone call.

Brooke was shaken up by everything—the shooting, the police, and the reason she was even at the shelter. She needed to escape the horror of the domestic abuse.

Five minutes later, the FBI arrived and informed Brooke that they were taking her to safety elsewhere.

CHAPTER 2

On the ride to FBI headquarters, Brooke was told to remain calm and not to ask questions. She was informed that she would soon be briefly meeting with Agent Miller and would be able to ask questions at that time.

The only question Brooke was asked during the ride was if she was hungry. Brooke replied, "Yes," and she said that she was tired too.

Agent Scott told Brooke that she would be well taken care of at headquarters.

The vehicle was between two other FBI cars. One car was in front of the car she rode in, and one car was behind her car.

Brooke's mind was spinning. The three-hour trip felt like an eternity. The car slowed down, turned left, and eased through a gate.

The driver of the car ahead appeared to show the guard a badge. The gate opened, and the first car entered. It abruptly closed as the car Brooke was in approached the guard. The driver displayed his badge, and the gate reopened. They entered a long, winding road lined with pine trees.

The sun had not yet risen when the three cars stopped outside a brick building. Several guards stood outside another checkpoint at the entrance. Agent Scott swiped his badge, and a steel door opened. Brooke was led inside and was introduced to Agent Miller. He shook her hand and offered her a seat inside a conference room.

Brooke let out a sigh and began to relax a little.

Agent Miller thanked her for being so cooperative and offered her flavored water and a cream cheese bagel. Brooke ate small bites as Agent Miller began asking questions.

After she had answered a few questions, Agent Miller told her that the crime she had witnessed was under investigation. They would need to question her further. After she got some rest, he would follow up.

At ten o'clock, there was a knock on her door. A woman wheeled a cart into the room with Brooke's breakfast.

"Thank you."

"You're welcome."

As the woman began to leave, Brooke said, "Where am I? Can I call my family?"

The woman told Brooke that someone would be meeting with her soon.

After breakfast, there was another knock at the door. A stern man told her to follow him down the hall.

She did as she was told and was motioned into an office. Inside the office, Agent Miller was with four other agents. Agent Miller explained that she had witnessed a highly sensitive and top-secret crime. She was a target of the criminals because they had a full description of her.

Agent Miller put his hand on her arm and said he was sorry to inform her that she would be entering the witness protection program. Brooke would have no contact with anyone from her past life—and she would have to change her name and identity.

CHAPTER 3

Maisie was Brooke's new name. She wasn't too sure if she liked the name, although she had no choice in the matter. Three months had passed since the morning of the crime. Maisie attended daily training sessions for the witness protection program.

Maisie was a serious person with a humorous side. When Maisie was informed that she would be employed at Harvest Moon Shop as a store clerk, she said, "I wish finding employment was that easy when I was Brooke. It took me a year to find a job before."

The trainer that day was Eileen Harper. Although Eileen found Maisie's humor delightful, she was forced by the rules to tell her not to ever mention the name Brooke when referring to herself. Training was rigorous and detailed. Because of all the extensive changes Maisie had to undergo, she met with a psychiatrist after each training session. The FBI staff told her that she was not being brainwashed; she was being transformed.

Maisie learned every detail about her new life. She was single, thirty-three years old, and had a father, a mother, and a younger brother. She would work at Harvest Moon and live with her parents. Her brother Dominick lived in a nearby town with his wife and two sons. They were all Catholic, which Maisie knew little about. Learning the faith was part of her daily training.

Maisie said, "Dr. Foreman, I feel as though I will be living a lie."

Dr. Foreman nodded and said, "Maisie, do yourself a favor and begin thinking as Maisie. Don't let your past consume your mind. Soon it will become second nature to live as Maisie." Dr. Foreman prescribed medication to ease the transition.

It was a hard not to think about the past. She had a father, mother, siblings, and friends as Brooke. She loved them dearly and had pride in her former existence, but they were to never be talked about or seen again.

Maisie began thinking about her new life. Dr. Foreman had been right. After daily training and memorizing documents full of details about her new life, thinking as Maisie became second nature. The time had come to put her new life into place.

CHAPTER 4

Maisie's new parents were somewhat snobbish. They lived in a large home in a wealthy community. The brick house had white pillars, a long porch, and many windows. Each house in the quiet neighborhood sat on an acre of land.

Bob and Donna were a bit disgraced that Maisie was a clerk at a shop that sold mystic items, Buddha dolls, and healing stones, but it was part of the act. Bob, Donna, Dominick, and his wife all had training before bringing Maisie into their lives. They had been given a large amount of money for agreeing to their new lives as well. Only their closest friends and relatives knew about Maisie's role in the witness protection program.

The rooms were large and had oriental rugs and high-quality furniture. A beautiful crystal chandelier hung above the long glass dining room table. There was a big television in the living room and a large spiral staircase in the hallway. Maisie's large bedroom was her retreat—a place to put up her feet, relax, listen to music, and shed some tears. She missed her old life. She missed her real mom and dad, and she was sure they missed her too. She wondered how they were handling her disappearance.

During her three months of training, Maisie was informed that she had been listed as a missing person. She thought her real parents, Abe and Judith, must be heartbroken. She wondered if posters had been placed around her hometown and assumed that the story of her disappearance had been on the news. She would never know the answers. She would only be able to assume.

Maisie met monthly with a psychiatrist from her new community. Her sessions with Dr. Stockton were the only time she could talk about her true feelings about the life she missed. Dr. Stockton knew about her involvement in the witness protection program. He consented to signing agreements and adhering to the utmost confidentiality. Dr. Foreman had been right about the life of Maisie becoming second nature, but the memories lingered. Dr. Stockton found this to be natural and showed no concern about Maisie's dilemma.

Maisie was a strong woman with good intentions and a loving heart. She had a charming personality that people were drawn toward. She had been trained to control her emotions on a day-to-day basis. She even attended acting classes during her training. Maisie trained herself to smile more as she peered into her bedroom mirror during her training.

She worked at Harvest Moon every day but Sunday and Monday. Maisie drove a run-down, two-door sedan. She earned minimum wage plus an extra fifty cents per hour. Her life was uneventful.

Her new state was warmer, and snow rarely fell. Snow was one of the few things she didn't miss.

On her way to work one day that fall, her front left tire blew. As Maisie looked at the blown tire, a sports car pulled over and a handsome man stepped out. He was wearing a dark gray suit with a tasteful purple tie. He was tall and had dark hair.

Maisie almost forgot she had a car problem.

"Need help?" the man asked.

Maisie replied, "If you wouldn't mind, yes. But you don't want to ruin your suit, do you?"

The handsome man smiled and said, "I'm Emmett. Nice to meet you."

Maisie said, "Thank you. It's nice to meet you too, Emmett."

Emmett asked if she had a spare tire and gladly changed the tire as they exchanged small talk. He gave Maisie his phone number after the spare tire was on her car.

It had possibly been the best day of her life.

CHAPTER 5

The following day, Maisie met with Dr. Stockton. Her appointments with him were at the same time every Thursday.

Dr. Stockton informed Maisie that he had an agenda. The first topic was to inform Maisie that she would soon be meeting with a licensed therapist on Wednesdays. He had realized that he was not educated enough about domestic abuse, and he thought that Maisie would benefit from therapy with someone who specialized in that area.

Maisie agreed, but she wondered in the back of her mind if her car would make it to work and back each day in addition to therapy on Wednesdays and psychiatrist appointments every Thursday. She could use extra help in sorting her thoughts and feelings. Maisie had never dealt with the abuse from her past, but she was open and willing to obtaining help from a therapist. Like Dr. Stockton, the therapist would adhere to confidentiality agreements.

The next topic on Dr. Stockton's agenda was her day-to-day life and how she felt she was handling the changes. Maisie began by discussing her physical appearance, which had been altered during the training. Her hair, which was previously short but stylish, had grown and not been cut. The style had been altered, and the color was changed from blonde to dark brown with highlights. In her former life, she typically wore sweatshirts and jeans. A stylist brought Maisie an entirely new wardrobe. The shirts were fashionable even though they looked like they had been made in the 1960s. Most of the shirts had flower prints, and she wore bell-bottom jeans.

Maisie surprised Dr. Stockton by saying that she liked the changes to her physical appearance. She was losing weight every week. She had been seventy pounds overweight before. She liked her hair at its new length and color. The choice of clothing was beginning to grow on her. Dr. Stockton was pleased with Maisie's progress. She was adjusting to the abundant changes at a normal pace.

The last part on the agenda was set aside for Maisie to ask questions or discuss anything she wanted to. Maisie said she had nothing to discuss. Dr.

Stockton asked her to dig deep within and tell him what she felt. Maisie sat still for a moment and thought about how her mind was organizing all the information. She was happy about that, but she knew she needed to do some soul-searching about how she felt deep inside. "I'm angry and happy at the same time," she said.

Dr. Stockton smiled and said that he would see her next week.

That evening, Maisie sat dazed in front of the television. Her mom and dad wondered what her mind was consumed with. Maisie was thinking about all the events of her day. Her shift at Harvest Moon had been easy. She would soon be meeting with a therapist, and she felt a sense of anticipation about dealing with the abuse from her former boyfriend. Maisie sorted all her thoughts of day and focused her thoughts on the best part of her day—meeting Emmett. She had already memorized his phone number. She studied it at work when there were no customers. Maisie wondered when she should call him. She didn't want to call that night and appear anxious, yet she didn't want to wait too long and appear uninterested. She decided that the following day would be the right time to call.

The news broadcasters reported about the day's events, which were mostly crime stories. Maisie began thinking about the crime she had witnessed. It was something she thought about often. She knew the crime had more significance to the law enforcement officers than solving a shooting, but she was never given the details about the crime for her own protection. She knew she was better off not knowing the details, but that didn't stop her mind from wondering about it every once in a while.

Maisie's mom suggested that she get something to eat for dinner. Thursday was labeled "fend for yourself night" at home. No one was cooking dinner or ordering dinner in. Thursday nights were set aside to find leftover food and making their own meals. On the other nights, they took turns cooking dinner. They all got along well. Bob and Donna had deep empathy for Maisie's circumstance, although it was never discussed. It was a new life for Maisie, and it was an opportunity to live life in a positive direction.

Maisie spent the following day thinking about her phone call to Emmett. She decided that she would call him after dinner. The evening was her time to relax and wind down from the day. At seven o'clock, Maisie got her nerve up to make the call. She had rehearsed what she would say and how she would say it. She had never been starstruck by a man before. She did not want to make a mistake or say anything that would turn him away.

Maisie stared at her phone's contact list. She saw Emmett's name and decided not to think about it any longer. She took the plunge and called him.

"Hello?" Emmett said.

"Hello, Emmett. This is Maisie—the girl you changed the tire for."

Emmett laughed and said, "Maisie, you don't need to explain who you are. First of all, you're the only Maisie I have ever met. Second, you're the only person whose call I've been anticipating since we met."

They talked as though they had known each other forever. There was an instant connection—and a bit of love at first sight.

Emmett and Maisie began forming a bond that was the start of their foundation. While trying to decide where to meet on their first date, Emmett suggested a local playground. Maisie was a bit taken aback. Emmett informed Maisie that he had a daughter—but he was not married. She was the child of his first girlfriend. They were no longer a couple. In fact, Emmett's former girlfriend was married to someone else.

Maisie was surprised. The thought never entered her mind that he would already be a father. She knew she had to say something quickly. "Are you sure you want to introduce me to your daughter already?"

Emmett had no concerns that a relationship with Maisie would not work out. He had the utmost confidence that she was the one for him. "She'll love you. Meet us at one o'clock tomorrow."

Maisie agreed.

They said their good-byes and hung up. Maisie was still very much in awe of Emmett, but his having a daughter was something she was not prepared for. In her former life as Brooke, she was the youngest child in her family and was not accustomed to dealing with children. She had worked an office job in her former life and rarely spoke to children. She liked children, but she had limited experience with them.

On Saturdays, Maisie only worked for four hours in the morning. The store closed at noon, which gave her a chance to meet Emmett and his daughter at the playground. She was still trying to familiarize herself with her new community. She knew all the main roads—but not the side streets. She wished she had a built-in GPS in her old Ford. She looked up the directions on her phone and pulled into the playground parking lot with a great amount of confidence. Maisie didn't want to act as though she was unfamiliar with the territory, and she wanted to present herself as a confident woman.

Maisie spotted Emmett immediately. He was hard to miss. His charm and good looks stood out from everyone else who was there. Emmett was pushing his young daughter on the swings. She had brown hair, brown eyes, and an outfit that looked like it was new.

Maisie approached them and said hi to Emmett.

Emmett turned toward Maisie with a big grin. "Maisie, this is Alexandria. We call her Alex for short."

Maisie smiled and said, "Hi, Alex. It's nice meeting you."

Alex smiled and then asked her dad to push her faster.

Emmett pushed Alex on the swing while Maisie and Emmett chatted.

"You have a beautiful daughter," Maisie said.

"Thank you, Maisie," Emmett replied.

Alex wanted to climb on the slide.

Maisie spotted a flower on Alex's shirt and said, "We're matching. We both have flowers on our shirts."

Alex had a big smile on her face and ran over to the slides.

Emmett and Maisie followed close behind. Maisie felt a stranger staring at her. She got that type of attention from men occasionally, but something did not feel right about this man. He was standing beneath a tree. He was not at the playground with any children and immediately walked away. He wore a dark blue baseball cap, a dark shirt, jeans, and brown boots. She guessed he was in his thirties. When she caught up to Emmett, she told him about the stranger.

Emmett looked toward the bench, but the man was nowhere to found. Emmett told Maisie that everything was fine.

Emmett, Maisie, and Alex spent an hour at the playground and went out for ice cream.

"You have a knack with kids," Emmett said.

"Thank you," she said.

Although Maisie's first date with Emmett wasn't what she had hoped for, it turned out to be wonderful. Maisie was beginning to truly like her new life.

CHAPTER 6

On Wednesday, Maisie went to meet her new therapist. The office was near Dr. Stockton's office. The buildings all looked the same. She checked in at the front desk and took a seat in the waiting area. As she glanced at the other patients, she noticed a man who looked familiar. Maisie thought she knew him from somewhere, but she couldn't think of where. She assumed that he must have been a customer at Harvest Moon. It was gnawing at her, but she let it go.

When her name was called, she stood up. Her new therapist introduced herself as Karen.

Maisie sat down in Karen's office, and Karen explained that her main purpose was to help Maisie deal with the abuse. However, the first session was just to get to know one another. It was the beginning of a long journey. They talked about Maisie's life. She told Karen about her mom, dad, brother, sister-in-law, and nephews.

Karen spoke a little about her life so that Maisie felt comfortable and would begin gaining trust in her. After thirty minutes, the session was over. Maisie was impressed with Karen. She had two college degrees and a therapy license. Karen was thirty-five, married, and had a boy and a girl. Maisie felt a bit of jealousy that Karen's life had not been altered like Maisie's life had been, but it did not get in the way of the therapy.

The following day, Maisie met with Dr. Stockton. She told him that she liked Karen. Dr. Stockton and Maisie discussed her past life and the feelings she stored inside. Maisie's head was adjusting to her new life, but her emotions were not. Dr. Stockton's job was to help Maisie align her head with her emotions, which took numerous sessions.

Maisie drove home after her appointment and blared the music in her car. She loved classic rock. Suddenly, she remembered the patient in the waiting room. She would not forget his eyes. He was the criminal from the alley.

As soon as she walked in the front door, Maisie rushed up to her bedroom and called the police. When they arrived, Maisie explained that she needed to speak to the FBI. She no longer had any contact with them. They had severed all ties with her for her protection. They kept watch on her house and drove by her workplace every once in a while, but she had not been given the witness protection program training location or phone numbers.

The police wondered if she had a mental issue until she mentioned Agent Scott, Agent Miller, and several other agents she had met in the training program. The police connected her to the FBI on speakerphone. Everyone at the FBI knew Maisie's name.

Agent Anderson immediately said that Maisie was credible and commanded Officer Ryan to bring her to the police department where the FBI agents would talk to her.

When Maisie arrived at the police department, Agent Scott was already there. He greeted Maisie and brought her into an office.

Maisie informed Agent Scott that she had seen the criminal, but Agent Scott thought Maisie was mistaken. She insisted it was the same man. Agent Scott removed himself from the room and called Agent Miller.

Agent Miller instructed Agent Scott to bring her back to FBI headquarters for questioning. She met with a group of agents.

Agent Miller said, "It's been a while, Maisie. We thought we would not need you to come back here again. Would you mind speaking to us about what you claim to have seen?"

Maisie sat down and told them what she had seen.

Agent Miller showed Maisie a book of mug shots. Within thirty seconds, she pointed to the right man.

"Hawk," Agent Miller said to his staff. Hawk was a hardened criminal who was on the run. The FBI thought he was in Mexico, but they grew concerned about his whereabouts. They were concerned about Maisie's safety.

Maisie was stunned and angry. She wanted to scream and ask why they had changed her identity if he was going to find her anyway. She caught her breath and said, "I thought I was safe. I thought the witness protection program was going to keep the criminals from finding me."

Agent Miller said, "Maisie, we do our best job here, but one thing we don't do is make 100 percent guarantees. Nothing in life is a guarantee. It's a hard lesson to learn, but you might as well learn it now."

Maisie thought his words were a bit harsh.

Agent Miller said, "We're going to keep you here until we feel safe about allowing you to return to your new home."

Maisie was upset. She just wanted to live a normal life. She wanted to go to work every day and come home every day. And she wanted to date Emmett. "Will I be allowed to contact people from my current life?"

Agent Miller said, "Not at this time. No, you cannot."

Massie didn't know whether to scream or cry. A tear formed in her eye.

"I'm sorry, Maisie. It's for your own safety and well-being."

Maisie was led to a room where she would stay until things were worked out. She knew Emmett would wonder what had happened to her.

After a few days, Maisie poured her heart out to them. She said she desperately wanted to live a normal life and was willing to take the risk of Hawk finding her again.

The FBI wasn't too keen on the idea, but after an hour, they decided to allow her to go home. Agent Miller was against it, but his bosses made the final decision.

When Maisie got home, Bob and Donna were on the couch. They had been informed about the incident.

She felt a sense of relief that they already knew.

Bob let her know that her job was safe. He had notified the owner.

She was still worried about Emmett. She checked her phone to see if he had tried contacting her. His last text said that he was worried about her. Maisie texted him and said she was okay.

Emmett called and they talked for two hours. They had a second date at a nice restaurant—just the two of them. Maisie thought it was worth the risk of Hawk finding her again. She had been through so much in her life that even short, happy moments meant everything to her.

CHAPTER 7

Weeks and months passed by. Emmett told Maisie that he had fallen in love with her. Maisie said the same to him. Alex grew fond of Maisie. The world could not be brighter for them. Maisie learned a lot about Emmett, including that he was a high-level music manager. He had an office in a high-rise in the city, but he did most of his work from home. He managed his time so that their work hours were about the same, which gave them a lot of time together. Emmett and Maisie spent almost all of their free time together.

Maisie was happy and living the normal life she had always wanted.

One day at Emmett's house, he sat down on the couch next to Maisie. He looked at her with love, placed his hand in hers, and said, "Honey, how would you feel about moving in with me?"

Maisie's heart skipped a beat. She thought for a moment, nodded, and smiled.

"Is that a yes?" Emmett asked.

"Yes, it is, sweetheart," Maisie replied.

CHAPTER 8

I would have to break the news to Bob and Donna. I was going to be moving in with Emmett. As I walked in the front door, I hung my keys on the key rack and set down my purse. My mother was in the kitchen. I wasn't sure where my dad was. "Hello," I said.

Donna looked happy to see me and said, "Hello, Maisie." My parents hugged me every time I returned home. In fact, they hugged everyone they knew who entered their home. I wasn't used to that in my former life, but I was aware that some families were like that.

Bob and Donna were practicing Catholics and attended church every Sunday. Both of them encouraged me to go with them since being Catholic was part of my new identity. I politely refused all but a few times. For some reason, I had trouble remembering the specific gestures that people made during Mass. It made me feel out of place, but I had a spiritual feeling whenever I walked inside the church.

"Where's Dad?" I asked.

"Still at work." Bob was an executive at a large car manufacturing company. "He had to fire someone today, so he might seem a bit on edge when he gets home."

I never really thought about the downside of his job. I was usually more focused on the luxuries Bob and Donna had: the expensive, well-kept home, his executive position, and the stocks and money. Bob watched the stock market reports on the news every night while we ate dinner. The bookshelves were filled with books about investing money, the stock market, and real estate. All the books were hardcover. None of them were paperback. It made me wonder if the books were there for display purposes or if they were really read.

Even though Bob and Donna came across a bit snobbish toward others, they were good people. After all, they had taken me into their home to aid in my protection. It was hard to get to really know them at first, but after a while, I realized they were reliable and caring people.

My brother also worked at the plant as a manager in the assembly line. Dominick worked hard for his money, and he was a good husband and father. He lived in the town next to mine. That was helpful since Donna often babysat his two sons. Donna babysat at Dominick's house because she didn't want a mess in our home.

Nothing was out of place at home. In fact, one room was roped off to keep the grandsons from going inside. The room had white walls, an off-white rug, and a white grand piano. I never saw anyone playing it. I questioned Donna about the piano one day. I asked if she or Bob knew how to play it. Donna said that both of them knew how. If I knew how to play the piano, I would not let an expensive grand piano go unused in my living room. Things like that were typical with Bob and Donna. They had expensive items that were never used. I believe their image was more important to them than actually enjoying the things they had.

Donna liked expensive clothes and jewelry. She spent most of her free time at high-end department stores. Many times, she shopped with her daughter-in-law. Jillian had the same expensive taste. The two of them got along well, and Dominick got along well with Bob. They had work in common, and they liked the same football team.

Even though the family welcomed me and treated me as one of their own, I still felt a bit out of place. Although that was not the reason I was going to be moving in with Emmett. I was moving in with him because I wanted to strengthen our relationship.

When Bob got home, he did not seem on edge. During dinner, I broke the news that I would be moving in with Emmett the following day.

Bob extended his hand and said, "Congratulations."

Donna looked as though I was intentionally rejecting living in their home—as if I had a personal grievance with them. She smiled slightly and said nothing.

Later that night, I had a long talk with Donna. I assured her that there was nothing personal against the family. I was leaving to be with the man of my dreams. After an hour or so, Donna said she fully understood.

CHAPTER 9

I was so in love. Things were definitely moving in the right direction for me. I went to work and had an appointment with Dr. Stockton.

When I arrived at Harvest Moon at ten o'clock, it was still closed. As I walked up the steps, I turned the doorknob and peered through the window. It was dark inside, and the door was locked. I was never in charge of opening the store, and I wondered which employee had been scheduled to open that day.

A car pulled into the parking lot next to mine. Amanda looked frazzled and out of breath as she stepped out of her car. Her purse kept slipping off of her shoulder while she walked as fast as she could toward the door. "Ugh. A bit late today. Have you been waiting long?"

"No," I replied, "I just got here. Are you okay?"

We were about the same age. Amanda was the closest friend I had since my transformation to Maisie.

Amanda said, "It's my dad, Maisie. He had a massive heart attack last night. I just left the hospital."

I looked at her with shock and empathy and told her to go home and get some rest. "I will run the store. Don't worry."

"Thank you, Maisie. I owe you one," Amanda said as she unlocked the door.

It was dark inside, and I was alone. I wasn't even sure where the lights were. I had never been in charge of opening the store.

After several minutes, I figured it out. I plugged in the "Open for Business" sign, and a few customers came into the store. They made small purchases and left. It was a typical day until a strange-looking older woman entered the store. She was slightly hunchbacked and dressed in black with a purple poncho. We were the only two people in the store. She browsed for a few minutes, touching the healing stones and admiring a four-leaf clover that was encased in a lucky coin. I asked how she was, and she replied, "Just fine. Do you believe in magic?"

I hesitated and said, "Well, yes. Of course." I wasn't really sure about my answer. I worked in a shop that was geared toward items for people who believed such things—the type of people who believed in spiritual things like psychics, mediums, magic, voodoo, and the zodiac.

"Very good, dear." She put three crystals on the counter and asked me what my name was.

"Maisie."

"Maisie, do you see these three crystals? Each one has a special power. I am going to explain each one to you."

The first crystal was light blue. "This holds the power of significance," she said. "October 23—remember today."

"Okay," I said. "But why?"

"Because it is the date of significance." She picked up the second crystal, which was golden.

I looked at the crystal and then looked up at her.

"Opportunity," she said.

I remained silent and looked at her.

"Young lady, you are a gift from God. We all walk with the power of opportunity, but you possess one unique opportunity—the opportunity of connection. The power to feel and sense real things that are beyond your reach. Use it wisely."

As I listened to her words, my head scrambled to make sense of it all. I immediately wondered what she would say about the third crystal. The third crystal was as black as the darkest night.

The old woman asked me for the total cost and motioned for me to get a shopping bag.

As she began walking toward the door, my curiosity got the best of me. I opened my mouth and said, "Ma'am, what's that black crystal all about?"

She slowly turned toward me and said, "Mysteries. Mysteries of life. Never forget they exist."

I nodded, and she left the store. She had given me a lot of food for thought, but I didn't have much time for that. My shift was nearly over, and I had an appointment with Dr. Stockton.

CHAPTER 10

Amanda went home to get some rest. She was married and had two children. Her husband was at the front door when Amanda walked in. She knew immediately that something was wrong.

Neil said, "We need to go back to the hospital, Mandy."

Amanda had felt weary before she opened the door, but after seeing the serious look on Neil's face, adrenaline took over her body. Suddenly, Amanda was walking and talking like there was no tomorrow. The possibility was strong that there would be no tomorrow for her dad.

Neil had already sent their two children to be taken care of by his parents while they returned to the hospital. In the intensive care unit, Amanda's family had gathered. They appeared anxious, tired, and sad.

"How is he, Mom?" Amanda asked.

Amanda's mother was speechless.

Amanda's uncle approached and said, "Mandy, your father is holding on."

"Why can't we see him? And why is everybody in the waiting room?"

"He's in bad shape, sweetie. The doctor has been allowing us to see him every once in awhile—but only two people at a time."

Amanda immediately felt weak. She looked around and saw an unoccupied seat. Amanda asked the woman next to it if it was taken.

The woman told Amanda that she was waiting for news about her daughter. Her daughter had been in a coma for months.

Amanda was about to tell the woman about her dad, but a doctor walked in and told Amanda's family that her father had died.

The family gathered closer, cried, and talked with one another.

Amanda got up to join them, and the woman next to her said, "I'm sorry for your news, dear."

Amanda said, "Thank you. Best of luck to you and your family with your daughter."

The woman replied, "Thank you dear."

Amanda's family asked the doctor a few questions as they consoled one another. After an hour, everyone from her family had left the hospital. Funeral arrangements had to be made. Amanda offered to assist her mother with the dreadful task. She and Neil went home. It had been a long day for everyone.

CHAPTER 11

My appointment with Dr. Stockton went well. In fact, he informed me that I was doing so well that I would begin seeing him only once a month and not every week. He had also lowered the dosage of my medication two weeks earlier. I had been on medication to help ease the transition from Brooke to Maisie. Dr. Foreman had originally prescribed the medication, but Dr. Stockton had continued it.

Dr. Stockton asked how my therapy sessions were going with Karen. I told him that they were going well and that she had educated me about important lessons in life. For example, I learned the value of counting my blessings every day. I had been through so much in my life, but I learned to appreciate what I had and not to focus on what had been taken from me—my identity. I learned to think about the fact that things could be worse. I could be living in a foreign land with no water or food. I could be dead. I could have no one who cared about me.

I learned to appreciate everyone who took the time to care—even paid professionals such as Dr. Stockton and Karen. Bitterness entered my mind occasionally. I would think about the fact that Dr. Stockton and Karen were being paid to care about me, but I didn't entertain that thought for too long. I turned it around and realized that if I didn't have their care, I didn't want to think about where I would be at that point. I kept thinking positive thoughts. I appreciated that they were there for me. I appreciated my family and friends—and I appreciated Emmett.

After my session with Dr. Stockton was over, I made it as far as the waiting room before my phone lit up.

Amanda said, "Maisie, my dad died."

I said, "I'm so sorry, Amanda. Is there anything I can do?"

"Just be there for me."

I told her I would always be there for her and that she was my best friend. I did not want to disturb the patients in the waiting room. I went outside and finished our conversation in my car. We talked for about fifteen minutes. I was never really sure what to say to someone who was dealing with the death of a loved one, but I think I did all right with Amanda. I let her do most of the talking, and I spent most of the conversation just listening to her. She was interrupted and had to say good-bye. She told me she would call later. She had to help her family with the funeral arrangements.

I told her to let me know when the funeral was so that I could attend. She said she would have the information that night.

When I arrived home, I went right to the kitchen. It was fend-for-yourself night.

Bob was watching television on the couch as he ate his dinner. Donna was resting her feet on an ottoman as she ate. They were happy to see me. We chatted for a couple of minutes, but I really wanted to go up to my bedroom, eat my dinner, and reflect on the day.

When I got to my room, I set my dinner plate and glass of water on my desk. I kicked off my shoes and put on my comfortable moccasins. I ate dinner at my desk and then retreated to my bed. My headphones were on my pillow. I had been listening to music that morning. I moved them aside and rested my head on my pillow.

I looked out my window as and thought. It was beginning to get dark, and it looked cold. After a few minutes, I remembered I was moving into Emmett's house the following day. I checked my phone. There were three texts from him: "Hello, my love," "You there, baby?" and, "Hi, baby. Call me when you see this."

I didn't hesitate to call. We talked about my moving arrangements. He would be at my home on Friday night to help move my things. We said our romantic good-byes, and I smiled. He always made hard days feel joyous.

I thought about the old woman in the store and the crystals. I tried to piece it all together, but I could not figure it out. *Maybe there is no meaning to it all. Maybe she was just a crazy lady. That must be it.* The mystery crept through my brain until I finally fell asleep.

CHAPTER 12

On Friday, I was excited to move into Emmett's house. He was the man of my dreams and beyond. I had to go to work first. The owner knew Amanda's dad had died and allowed her to have a few days off from work.

When I arrived at ten o'clock, the owner had opened the shop. Charlie was an elderly man with gray hair, a gray mustache that was a bit too long, and wrinkles. He looked like someone who had worked hard all of his life, but he still had an energetic spirit. He would sometimes tell jokes that I found inappropriate, but I laughed anyway. I realized it was just a small part of who he was. I got to know him as someone who would give a person in need the shirt off his back. He was kind and generous, and he was a good person to work for. Charlie was very understanding. His shop didn't earn him a fortune, but he gave Amanda the time off with pay.

Charlie and I worked together. We took turns for our lunch breaks. During his turn, he left the store for an hour. I got a big surprise when Emmett showed up. He was on his lunch break and wanted to see me because he missed me. We were so in love with each other.

Emmett had never been inside Harvest Moon. He looked around at the merchandise. I had a customer at the register, and I spent a few moments cashing her out. I turned my back from the counter for a second to reach for a shopping bag and heard a knock. The customer was standing to the side, and a fuzzy stuffed rabbit was peering at me from the counter. Emmett was squatting down with his arm extended. He was wearing a top hat that we sold in the store as part of a magic kit.

"Very funny," I said.

Emmett smiled and said, "You just witnessed a great magician pulling a rabbit out of a hat. This is your lucky day, ma'am."

The other customer laughed and smiled. "Cute trick." When she left the shop, I told Emmett I loved him. He always had a way to make me smile. He told me he loved me too, and we discussed a few minor details about the move.

Emmett had to return to his job after his lunch hour. Charlie had not returned, and I had no customers in the store. I called Amanda, and she sounded like she was handling the situation as well as she possibly could. Some of her family lived out of state, and they would be traveling for the funeral. She gave me the details about the funeral arrangements.

When Charlie returned to the store, I gave him details about the funeral. We called the other employees to let them know the funeral was scheduled for Monday. Charlie scheduled an employee who did not know Amanda that well.

Bob and Donna were sad to see me leave, but that they understood and wished me nothing but happiness. Dominick and Jillian were there to help. Robin and Edison (ages eight and five) spent time with their grandma and grandpa, and the rest of us transported my belongings. Dominick and Emmett got along well despite their vastly different styles and personalities. Dominick was a jeans and T-shirt type of man; Emmett was more of a well-dressed, shirt and tie type. Emmett was not adamant about his clothing. He usually dressed for the occasion. Since we were moving my things, Emmett was dressed in a sweatshirt and jeans. Dominick had a nice, easygoing personality. His priorities were beer and football. Jillian had short, well-styled blonde hair. She was thin and dressed well for any occasion. She acted like a snob most of the time. I sometimes wondered if she married my brother for his money, but I liked giving people the benefit of the doubt—and I hoped that wasn't the reason. I got along well with Jillian, but she wasn't someone I wanted to spend a lot of time with.

We drove back and forth with my belongings, using my car and Dominick's truck. Emmett was surprised by how much I owned. I was ready to hear a snide comment about how women pack too much, but Emmett didn't say a word about it. He was a gentleman. I suppose I was waiting for a comment because relatives from my old life might have said something like that.

After the move, Emmett and I hugged and kissed. He said, "Welcome home, my sweet love."

I smiled from ear to ear. It was a nice place to begin the next level of our relationship.

CHAPTER 13

The funeral for Amanda's father was on Monday morning. Emmett and Maisie were there with Charlie. The funeral service was at the Methodist church. Even though Amanda had grown up in that faith, she didn't attend church very often. Amanda believed in God, but she also believed in fortune telling, voodoo, and astrology. Amanda's mother was never too happy about that; Amanda kept her distance from her mom as much as possible. Amanda's mom needed her, and Amanda did everything she could for her.

The air was bitter cold. Winter was right around the corner. Maisie was freezing on the walk from the car into the church.

Emmett told her that she should have dressed warmer.

Maisie replied, "I know. I haven't gotten it into my head that it's not summer anymore. I'm not prepared for this type of weather."

Maisie had met Amanda's father and talked with him a few times, but she was mainly at the funeral to support her best friend.

The church choir was singing before anyone spoke. There were also people playing the organ and violin. Maisie was impressed, but she found out later that it only happened rarely. Amanda's father had been very active in the church and was liked by many people at church and in the community.

The minister started by saying his condolences and then read some passages from the Bible. The church was packed. There wasn't an empty seat. Several people were standing in the back. Amanda's uncle went up to the podium and spoke for about twenty minutes about his brother. Five other family members and friends did the same. The funeral service lasted two hours. It was followed by a buffet lunch in the church basement.

Maisie and Emmett stayed until most of the people had filed out of the church. Before they left, Maisie gave Amanda a big hug and promised her that she would be there for her whenever she needed.

Amanda said, "Thanks, Maisie. And if I can ever return the favor, I'll do the same."

They said good-bye and walked toward the exit. The church was empty except for a man near the doors. He pointed to a pair of women's gloves and asked Maisie if they belonged to her.

Maisie looked at the gloves and said, "No, they're not mine."

The man was a church member and said that he had asked everyone who attended the funeral the same question, and no one had claimed them. The man told Maisie that she could have them.

Maisie thanked him and put on the gloves.

When Emmett and Maisie returned home, Maisie told him that God must have been watching out for her that day.

Emmett just smiled politely.

CHAPTER 14

Maisie and Emmett spent the weekend enjoying each other's company. Their house was green and had a small white porch. It was built in the 1950s, but Emmett kept it upgraded. The inside felt homey. It had wood floors and large rugs in each room. The furniture was tasteful. The colonial-style home had three bedrooms. Emmett and Maisie shared the master bedroom. One of the bedrooms was used for Emmett's office. The third bedroom was for Alex when she spent weekends there. Alex lived with her mom, stepdad, and baby brother. She spent every other weekend and some vacations at Emmett's house.

Having Alex around part of the time made Maisie think about having a child with Emmett—a child who would call her "Mom." Alex called Maisie by her name. Maisie started to think about the fact that she was getting older and wondered if Emmett had a desire for more children. Maisie decided it would be okay if she never had a child of her own. Alex was a blessing to her, and even though she wasn't called "Mom," she felt like one toward Alex.

Maisie helped Alex with her homework on the weekends, and they did chores together. As time went on, they did things as a family. That weekend, they went to the movies with Emmett. The three of them had a great weekend together.

CHAPTER 15

Maisie was glad the funeral was over and life was returning to normal. She went to work the next day. Charlie went at the store to unlock the doors, turn on the lights, and prepare for the day.

Charlie handed her a set of keys and told Maisie that he would be giving her the responsibility of opening the store in the mornings. He increased her hourly pay by twenty-five cents. She was earning minimum wage plus an extra seventy-five cents per hour.

Charlie told Maisie she'd be on her own that day since he had some business to attend to elsewhere. Maisie put her belongings in the back room, stood by the cash register, and waited for some customers. The door opened, and the bell above it rang as usual. It was the old woman who had purchased the crystals.

"Welcome," Maisie said.

The old woman said, "Thank you." She was wearing the same clothes and wandered around the store for fifteen minutes while Maisie attended to other customers.

The other customers left without purchasing anything.

The old woman carried something to the checkout counter and put the heavy magic links on the counter.

Maisie asked what she would be using the links for since they were typically used for magic shows.

The old woman said, "Maisie, these links represent all living creatures. We are all bonded to one another by forces that are not in view by the human eye. Wars develop within the world when a link is broken or disconnected. It must immediately be brought back together. The energy within these links is powerful."

Maisie replied, "I see."

The old woman headed for the door.

Maisie said, "Have a nice day."

CHAPTER 16

Tuesday was Maisie's birthday, but it was not her real birthday from her former life. It was the date that was on her birth certificate with her new identity. Maisie was turning thirty-four that day.

Emmett made sure it was a day she would not forget. Even though it was not the weekend, he invited friends and relatives over to surprise her that evening after work. The biggest surprise was waiting in the driveway. He had bought her a new car.

Maisie had no idea there was anything for her as she walked into the kitchen. She thought that Emmett might have made her breakfast, but he hadn't. She wasn't even sure where he was until he stepped inside the front door.

He wiped his shoes on the mat and said, "There's the love of my life."

Maisie was wearing her bathrobe and moccasins.

"Happy birthday, my love," he said.

Maisie's hair was going in all different directions, and she had no makeup on. "Thank you, my sweet love."

"Look outside," he said.

Maisie looked outside. "Oh, it snowed last night. It's pretty."

"No, look in the driveway, sweetheart."

A shiny silver sedan had a big sign that read: "Happy Birthday, Maisie." Emmett looked at her and said, "It's yours."

"Oh, wow, Emmett!"

"Go over and look at it, my love. It's yours. It's paid in full. There are no monthly payments—we don't owe a thing on it."

Maisie walked right over to the car. "Thank you so much, Emmett. Thank you. Thank you."

"You're welcome. Enjoy."

Maisie wanted to admire the car, but she had to get ready for work.

Emmett made breakfast while she got ready. By the time she came downstairs, a plate was on the table with eggs and hash browns, a side dish of mixed fruit, a small glass of orange juice, and a cup of coffee.

Maisie knew she would be late to work if she sat down to eat the breakfast, but she was hungry—and she knew he worked hard to make her happy. She called Charlie to let him know she was running a little late. Charlie was scheduled to work that day, but Maisie was supposed to unlock the doors and open the shop.

Charlie knew it was Maisie's birthday and agreed to get there early to open the store for her.

Maisie ate breakfast with Emmett. He had even placed a vase with a rose on the center of the table.

After breakfast, Emmett handed Maisie the keys. They kissed, and Maisie drove to work.

When she arrived at the shop, Charlie was talking to a customer. He broke away from his conversation to wish Maisie a happy birthday.

Maisie thanked him for opening the store on such short notice.

He told her it was not a problem and mentioned that Amanda would be returning to work the following day.

"So soon?" Maisie asked.

"I told her she could stay out a few more days, but she said she thought it was best if she got back into a normal routine."

Maisie didn't want to come across as though she was bragging, so she wasn't sure if she should share the news about her new car.

Charlie looked out the window. "New car?"

Maisie smiled and told him that it was a birthday gift from Emmett.

Charlie tried to be funny and asked what she had to do to pay Emmett back. He reached for Maisie's arm and led her toward the door. "Come on. Show me. I want to see it."

They went to the parking lot and admired the car's exterior and interior. When a customer pulled into the parking lot, they returned to the store.

Charlie unpacked some small shipments, and Maisie attended to the customers. It was an average day at the store. Charlie wanted to tell Maisie she could leave early, but he couldn't. The plan was for the surprise party to begin after her shift. If she went home too early, it would ruin the surprise.

When it was time for the store to close, Maisie got into her new car and cranked the radio. She and Emmett had texted a few times during the day, but Emmett never let on that there would be a surprise party when she got home.

Maisie noticed several cars parked along the road and figured someone was having a party. As soon as she opened the front door, her friends and family shouted, "Surprise!"

She saw Emmett, Alex, Bob, Donna, Dominick, Jillian, Robin, Edison, Charlie, Amanda, Neil, and a few other friends and family members. The house was decorated with balloons and streamers. Maisie's favorite music was playing in the background. Everyone wanted to rush outside to see her new car.

Dominick asked Maisie what she was going to do with her old car.

Emmett said, "Out to the highest bidder."

Dominick responded, "That old clunker? Probably gonna have to pay someone to take it."

Maisie said, "My old car may look run down, but it never has any problems."

Emmett laughed and said, "Uh, Maisie dear, how is it that we met each other?"

Maisie laughed and said, "Okay it had a problem one time."

They celebrated with dinner, cake, ice cream, and drinks. They left after the cake was served since most of them had to work in the morning.

Maisie's life had never been brighter.

CHAPTER 17

Karen and Maisie met to discuss Maisie's abuse.

Maisie let out a large sigh and relaxed her shoulders.

"How has your week been?" Karen asked.

"Stressful but manageable." Maisie spoke about her week for five minutes, and Karen asked her to describe her life as Raymond's girlfriend.

"Let's see, Raymond was very controlling toward me. He would tell me what I could and could not watch on television. If I didn't listen to him and changed the channel to something he didn't like, he would hit me. He was a perfectionist, and if I made even the smallest mistake, he would yell and scream at me. One time after I had done the laundry and put his clothes away, he yelled at me for not putting the clothes in perfect alignment. He trained me in the correct way. One time, he put a knife to my throat. He said that if I left him, he would kill my family. So I stayed. And one time—"

Karen said, "Maisie, let me start by saying that you did a very brave thing by seeking help. No one deserves that type of treatment. No one. I'm sure you have plenty of other stories to tell, and you can at another time. For now, let's focus on two things: you are not in that situation currently and you're a hero for escaping the abuse. I want to educate you on the subject of abuse so that you may begin to heal. I believe that education is the first step in the healing process."

Maisie quietly listened to Karen. She had never heard that she was a hero or that she was brave. Maisie began feeling better about herself. She had not been aware that she held deep feelings of belittlement and lacked self-confidence. Negative feelings began to surface like wildfire.

Karen said, "Maisie, let's begin by informing you that there are typical patterns of abusers. They use certain tactics to gain the trust of their victims and then manipulate and control them. You are not alone. Degrading their victims is one tactic. They do this so that their victims begin feeling worthless about themselves and then feel more needy of the abuser. There's a term called 'power and control.' The abusers are very crafty in the process that they use. I will teach you some of the different ways they do this. For example, they use money as way to control their victims."

The word *money* triggered thoughts about how Raymond had ruined her financially. "Ray told me where to buy things and what to buy. He told me to use my own money. He said my money was our money because we were going to get married. I never saw a cent of his money. If I said anything about it, or asked about his money, I would end up regretting it because he would physically abuse me if I had. I did as I was told. I was scared all the time. I felt like I was walking on eggshells with every word I said and every move I made. He scared me. He even showed me where he would bury my family if I left him. He gave me details that led me to believe he was serious. I was so scared."

Karen said, "You're a very strong woman, Maisie. You found the courage to leave that situation. Good for you. Let's keep our time today short. I think you need time to process a few things that we brought up."

Maisie agreed and nodded.

"We'll meet at the same time next Wednesday," Karen said. "Enjoy the rest of your day before the snow begins. I heard it's supposed to snow on Friday."

Maisie said, "I thought it didn't snow in the South. I never would have moved here if I had known."

Karen smiled, knowing that Maisie was joking.

CHAPTER 18

Friday was Harvest Moon's busiest day of the week. Charlie typically scheduled two people to run the store. Maisie and Amanda were working that day. They were glad about that. It gave them a chance to catch up on things.

For the first thirty minutes, no one was in the shop. Maisie peered out of the window, but the parking lot was empty. As Maisie headed toward the checkout counter, the bell rang. It was the old woman with her husband. He was about the same height as his wife, and he was wearing a knitted hat. The old man was using a cane, and his back was a bit hunched.

Amanda greeted the two customers with a big smile.

They smiled at Amanda as the old man browsed the store. He laughed and said, "Voodoo dolls!"

Amanda whispered, "Maisie, they shopped here before. The old woman is crazy. He puts up with her though. He must really love her."

The old woman admired the lucky penny with the four-leaf clover.

"She looks at that penny every time she's here," Amanda said.

The old woman picked up the penny and brought it to the counter. "Maisie, dear, how are you?"

Maisie said she was fine.

"And, Amanda, my dear, how are you?"

Amanda replied, "I'm fine as well. Will you be purchasing this today?"

"Yes, dear," she replied.

The phone rang, and Amanda answered the call.

Maisie stepped up to the cash register to process the old woman's purchase.

"Miracles," said the old woman. "They're in every aspect of our lives. Do you exist in this world, Maisie?"

"Well, yes. Of course I exist in this world."

The old woman said, "Then that is a miracle. Every living being in this world has been blessed with a miracle."

The old man paid for the lucky penny, smiled, and said, "Magic, voodoo, stones, hocus pocus."

Maisie let out a slight giggle as she finished her work at the register.

The couple left the store as new customers arrived.

Later that afternoon, Amanda said, "That woman is crazy with a capital C."

Maisie just smiled and said, "Oh, they looked so cute together. I bet she knits as a hobby. I bet she made that hat he was wearing."

Amanda agreed.

The weekend had approached, and the two were excited to go home and enjoy a couple of days with their families.

Maisie had to work Saturday morning, but she was still happy it was the weekend.

CHAPTER 19

Maisie drove home to be with Emmett and enjoy a nice weekend together. It was their weekend to have Alexandria over. Maisie and Emmett greeted one another with a kiss as soon as she walked in the front door.

"It's so good to be home. I love you," Maisie said.

"I love you too, sweetheart. You're my one and only," he said. Emmett was wearing a white dress shirt, a gray-striped tie, dark pants, and black dress shoes. He had just returned from a meeting.

"You look so charming," Maisie said.

"Not as charming, beautiful, and stunning as you do," he replied.

Maisie, for a brief moment, reflected on her life with Raymond. If Raymond had ever said those words to her, he would likely have an ulterior motive. She broke away from the thought instantly, realizing that Emmett's words were spoken with the utmost sincerity. She trusted Emmett more than she had ever trusted anyone. He was kind to her—and he was kind to everyone he encountered. He was an all-around nice man, handsome, and charming. She felt like she had hit the jackpot.

Emmett was just as much amazed by Maisie. He found her to be the most beautiful woman he had ever seen. No matter what she was wearing or how tired she was, she was absolutely beautiful. Nothing was a problem in their relationship. They never argued. Their personalities had slight differences, but they were very much alike. It was just the right mixture and chemistry to make it a nearly perfect relationship.

"Do you want to ride along with me or do you want to stay home and begin relaxing?" Emmett asked.

"No question about it," Maisie replied. "I want to be with the man I love as much as possible while he picks up his wonderful little girl."

Emmett replied that her comment was sweet and joked that she made a wise choice. He wanted to be with her as much as she wanted to be with him.

When Emmett and Maisie went to pick up Alex, her mother darted toward Emmett's car.

Emmett rolled down the car window.

"You're two weeks late on child support. No money, no visit," Stacey said.

Emmett said, "I'll have it for you by next Friday,"

"Send Alex out here now," he said.

After glancing at Maisie, Stacey sarcastically asked Emmett, "Can't do any better than that?"

Emmett responded, "All right—enough. I want my daughter out here now."

Stacey walked toward her house to get Alex.

Maisie had only heard good things about Stacey via Emmett and Alex. Emmett kept it that way on purpose. He did not believe in speaking poorly about the mother of his child in front of Alex. He did not want to tell Maisie about Stacey's true persona and arrogance. Stacey was a borderline evil woman, but she was a good mother. Emmett and Stacey never married because Emmett didn't love her. Their relationship had only lasted two months. A month after they broke up, Stacey informed him of her pregnancy.

Alex exited the front door with an old suitcase. Emmett wanted to help her, but he also wanted Alex to develop more independence. He knew the suitcase wasn't too heavy for her to carry. Alex had a big grin on her face as she approached the car. Her teeth were large and bright white, and she was missing a tooth. She looked like the happiest kid on the planet. Stacey was a good mother, and Emmett was an awesome dad. And she had Maisie in her life. Maisie and Alex got along like a teacher and a student. Maisie was like a mentor to Alex. She taught her things that she didn't learn in school—such as the names of different types of flowers—and Alex was always eager to learn.

They had a pleasant conversation during the short trip home. They played a game and told each other one thing that they liked about their week and one thing that they disliked about their week. Alex began by saying she liked getting a letter from her pen pal.

Maisie asked her about it. She wasn't aware that Alex had a pen pal.

"Yeah, he lived near me when we were little, but he moved away. His name is Sawyer."

Maisie chuckled because she still saw Alex as a little kid.

Emmett smiled too.

Alex said, "And I had to go to school." Emmett and Maisie laughed because they knew she said that to be funny even though there was some truth behind it.

Emmett told Maisie it was her turn.

Maisie thought for a moment and said, "I liked two of the customers I had in the store this week. A cute old couple. And I disliked having to go to a funeral this week. Okay, your turn, Emmett."

Emmett said, "Having my two favorite people in the whole world with me. This is what I like about my week. This moment right now." He agreed that the funeral was the part of the week he disliked.

It was a good way for them to bond.

Maisie ordered pizza for dinner. All three were having a great evening together, but Maisie had to cut the evening short. She had a four-hour shift at the store in the morning.

Emmett spent a little bit of father-daughter time with Alex after Maisie went to bed. They would have the entire morning together while Maisie was at work.

Alex went to her room and fell asleep, and Emmett watched a football game on television before he went to bed.

The next morning, Emmett surprised Maisie with breakfast. She was running late, but she had time to eat quickly. She felt badly that she couldn't spend more time enjoying the meal, but Emmett understood.

At work, Maisie reflected on the encounter with Stacey. Although she knew it was none of her business, she wondered why Emmett was late with the child support. She wondered if she was the cause. She wondered if she was too much of an added expense in Emmett's household. She and Emmett had made an agreement that Maisie would pay for the electricity and groceries. Emmett could not ask Maisie to contribute any more, but Maisie was beginning to wonder if that was enough. Everything she read about relationships said that money was the number one reason most couples fought. She did not want her relationship to end up as part of that statistic. Maisie vowed not to let money be a contributing factor in any arguments with Emmett. She wanted her relationship with him to be more like a team than two opponents in a boxing match. She had encountered the latter with Raymond—and she did not want anything like that to happen again.

By the time she returned home, Emmett and Alex were enjoying a game of cards. A light dusting of snow carpeted the lawn, so the two of them found entertainment indoors. Maisie found humor in how southern people dealt with a small amount of snow. A trace of snow seemed to be nearly a nightmare to them. She also found it to be an enlightening change from the rugged attitudes about snow from people in the North.

Emmett and Alex greeted Maisie. Alex asked if she wanted to join them in their card game, but Maisie said she was going to begin making dinner. She had planned an elaborate meal for the three of them. Maisie loved to cook, but she didn't do it often. When she did cook, the meals turned out superbly. Emmett enjoyed cooking as well. He allowed Maisie to make the meal so that Emmett and Alex could have more father-daughter time.

The meal was delicious and they enjoyed it as much as they enjoyed the rest of the weekend. By Sunday afternoon, it was time to take Alex back home. After Emmett and Maisie dropped her off at her house, they wound down at home.

Emmett mentioned how wonderful his family time was with them. It was the first time Maisie had heard Emmett refer to the three of them as a family. It sounded like the ringing of bells to her ears. It was a pleasant way to end the weekend.

CHAPTER 20

The week was going by quickly. On Wednesday, Maisie met with Karen. As she read a magazine in the waiting room, she glanced around at the other patients. It reminded her of Hawk. She thought about the eye contact she had with him in the alley and in Karen's waiting room. Maisie typically lived without fear. After all, she was in the witness protection program. Somehow, Hawk had fallen through cracks of the system. He had tracked down Maisie—even with her new identity.

The FBI chief made a rare apology to Maisie and assured her that it would not happen again. This incident brought an awareness to Maisie that the intelligence level of Hawk was extremely high and that he fit nowhere on the profile charts of a typical criminal. Maisie knew nothing was foolproof. She had been reminded at FBI headquarters that there were no guarantees for her safety, but they had reiterated that she didn't need to waste her time worrying about it. She was told to live a normal life as best as she could and let the authorities do the worrying. They insisted that she was being protected.

As Maisie continued to think about Hawk, Karen interrupted her. It was time for their appointment. Maisie placed the magazine on the table, stood up, and walked into Karen's office.

Karen asked Maisie about her week. Maisie spent a few moments talking about her job and home life. She briefly talked about Emmett. He was her favorite topic of discussion. Karen was always glad to hear how well she was being treated at work and home.

Karen handed Maisie a piece of paper. The paper had typed words with a heading that said, "Power and Control." Below the heading, there was a list. Karen asked Maisie to read the list aloud.

"Coercion and threats, intimidation, emotional abuse, isolation, minimizing, denying and blaming, using children, economic abuse, and male privilege," Maisie said.

"Okay," Karen said. "Now I want you to peruse the list again and tell me what you think about it."

Maisie glanced at the sheet and said, "Interesting."

Karen waited for Maisie to elaborate.

"It's interesting, but I'm not sure what it means."

"These are some behaviors that an abusive person will use toward their victims—a list of patterns they use to gain power and control over their victims."

Maisie nodded.

"Now, is there anything, after looking at this list, that you'd like to discuss?" Karen asked.

Maisie smiled and said, "Yes, Emmett."

"I mean about the past abuse you suffered, Maisie. Is there anything you want to talk about?"

"I'm beyond all that, Karen. It's interesting—and I like learning—but as far as needing to vent from the abuse of the past, there is no need." Maisie had been through so many changes in her life that were almost more than anyone could handle. She wanted to move on with her life and not dredge up the past.

Karen said, "The emotions from your past needed to surface and be dealt with in order to happily move on with your life."

Maisie nodded. She understood the logic in Karen's statement. "He degraded me all the time. I never realized how worthless I was feeling until the moment I left him. It was like breathing fresh air for the first time."

Karen said, "That was a good start to healing, but our time is up for the day."

Maisie drove home and thought about the session. By the time she was home and saw Emmett, her mind shifted back to her life. She felt happy at home with Emmett and wondered why she had to talk about the past. Maisie decided to talk to Dr. Stockton about it during her next appointment. In the meantime, life was good for Maisie. She felt happy and content.

CHAPTER 21

The weekend arrived, but it was not Emmett's weekend with Alex. Maisie and Emmett had the weekend to themselves. Emmett kept in contact with Alex on a daily basis. Even though Alex was young, Emmett made sure she had her own phone. It was a way for him to keep in daily contact with her, and he thought it was an important safety measure.

After Emmett and Maisie were settled in for the night, Emmett called Alex. "Hi, honey."

"Hi, Dad. What up?"

They both laughed.

Alex was always trying to get others to laugh.

"Just checking to see how you are today. Maisie's here. Do you want to say hello to her?"

"Sure."

Maisie reached for Emmett's phone. "Hi, Alex. I haven't talked to you all week. How's school going?"

"Good."

"Have you heard from Sawyer lately?"

Alex said, "I just gotten a letter from him. He's doing good. He invited me to California. He said we could go to Disneyland and stuff like that. But my mom said we'll see."

Maisie said, "That's great, Alex. I've never been there, but I've heard how much fun Disneyland is. I'm going to hand the phone back over to your dad now. Glad you're doing well. I'll see you next weekend."

After the phone call, Emmett asked Maisie if she'd like to go out to dinner.

Maisie, remembering that Emmett was late with the child support, said that she'd prefer to stay home for dinner. Besides, she had to work in the morning.

They cooked together and enjoyed a romantic evening.

Maisie said, "Is the amount of money I contribute to the household enough?"

Emmett laughed slightly and said, "It's all good."

"What about child support and what Stacey said?" Maisie asked.

Emmett said, "It's all good. Look, Maisie, I wasn't going to let you in on this at this point, but I'm speaking to a lawyer about custody. I was advised to stop making child support payments."

"But you told me you already have partial custody of Alex."

"Yes. That's right, but I want full-time custody. I know I can provide a better life for her. She needs me. I'm her dad."

It was a side of Emmett that Maisie had not seen. As an outsider, Maisie could see that Emmett was being selfish. His points about Alex's happiness were invalid. Maisie was confident that Alex was a happy child and was taken care of at her mother's house and Emmett's home. "This is about what's best for Alex—not what's best for Emmett," Maisie said. She was amazed that she had the courage to speak her mind like that toward Emmett. She felt it was worth the risk of losing him. She thought it was better to speak her opinions than to bottle them up for the sake of keeping a relationship.

Emmett and Maisie discussed the issue for a couple of hours. Toward the end of the conversation, Emmett realized that Maisie was right. In the beginning of the discussion, he asked if Maisie was trying to free up his time for her own sake. By the end of the discussion, Emmett felt guilty for even entertaining the thought. He realized Maisie was sincere. He felt as though he had fallen in love with Maisie even more.

The discussion brought them even closer. The evening was well spent, but Maisie had to go to bed. Emmett spent a little time reflecting on their conversation before bed. On Monday, he would call his lawyer and drop the case.

CHAPTER 22

On Saturday morning, Charlie greeted Maisie as she entered the door to begin her shift. Charlie was very energetic. It was apparent to everyone who knew him that he was living his dream. He had a sense of passion for operating and owning the store. Charlie began the business after he became a Buddhist. Every once in a while, he would mention something about Buddhism, but he never pressured anyone to study it.

Maisie had a strong desire to learn about different cultures, religions, and environments. When Charlie spoke about finding balance in life, Maisie intently listened. Maisie wanted to learn as much about the world as possible so she could eventually formulate her own opinions. Living in disguise made it more difficult to live by her own values, but Maisie counted her blessings everyday. She focused on what she had—and not on what she lacked.

Charlie wasn't married, but he had been for a short time in his twenties. Maisie wasn't sure if he dated, although there was a rumor that he was very fond of a woman who lived in his apartment complex. Charlie would probably have a thousand people at his funeral. Even Bob and Donna knew Charlie prior to Maisie's employment at his shop.

There were several customers that morning. Charlie was running a contest in the store. He asked her to tell each customer to complete a short form and put it in the box near the cash register.

"What's the prize?" Maisie asked.

"The opportunity to meet me and take me to dinner."

Maisie laughed.

"The real prize is fifty dollars' worth of store merchandise."

Maisie couldn't wait to go home to Emmett, but she counted her blessings that she even had a job.

CHAPTER 23

It was Emmett's birthday. I felt like I needed to give him something special after all he did for me on my birthday. I had a good amount of money in my savings account. I made sure to put a little from my paycheck into the account each week. I had also sold my old car. Even though it wasn't much, I put the money into the account. I had just enough to buy concert tickets to see Emmett's favorite band. The band was performing on the West Coast, and I reserved a room at a luxury hotel for a full week.

I took the day off from work and decided to surprise Emmett by showing up at his office. Although he worked at home most of the time, he spent every Wednesday at his office. I parked in the four-story garage and walked toward the building. My head started to pound, and my stomach felt sick. Emmett's office was on the top floor. The elevator made my headache worse.

When the doors opened, I showed my identification to the security officers and told them who I was there to see.

The security officers called Emmett to notify him that I was there. When I saw Emmett walking toward me, my head stopped pounding and my stomachache was gone. Emmett greeted me with a big smile, and I wished him happy birthday. I had never been to Emmett's office, and he gave me a short tour of the office area and the recording studio.

Emmett showed me all the recording equipment and told me to step up to the microphone. "Put the headphones on," he said.

My favorite song was playing, and I had the opportunity to sing as my voice was being recorded.

Emmett showed me how my song was edited. It was starting to feel like it was my birthday and not his. I told him I had a gift for him.

Emmett led me into his office, and I handed him a large envelope with a heart on it.

He smiled, gave me a kiss, and said, "Thank you, sweetheart." Emmett opened the envelope and opened the card. The concert tickets fell out. He picked them up and said, "Thank you."

"Emmett, read the card," I said.

Emmett read the card and said, "Honey, you shouldn't have. How could you afford a vacation for us and concert tickets?" I told him that I had been saving for a long time.

He was amazed.

Emmett and I went to a classy restaurant for lunch. We had a nice conversation as we ate.

I had an appointment with Karen, and he had to return to work. He thanked me, and we said our romantic good-byes.

CHAPTER 24

I drove to the medical complex and met with Karen. I told her about my week, and Karen said she had spoken to Dr. Stockton about my progress. The two thought I was doing great. I had spent months talking about the abuse. Karen said she thought it was time to focus on my current life and the future. I agreed. She gave me the option of continuing with therapy or not. I chose the latter.

We spent the rest of the appointment talking about my current life. She shared a little about her life too. Her two children were a handful, and she was taking a couple of classes online. She also volunteered with the homeless. It made me wonder if she would need therapy in the future. After all, she had a husband, two children, a full-time job, a volunteer job, and she was taking classes. But that was none of my business.

I told Karen about life with Emmett and Alex and my job. I told her it wasn't my career of choice, but I was content. I told her that Emmett and I would be going away on vacation soon. She was sure I could use the break.

CHAPTER 25

Emmett and Maisie packed their suitcases in the trunk of Maisie's car. While Emmett set the GPS, Maisie looked around the house to see if she forgot anything. Once she felt confident that the necessities had all been packed, they were on their way. Emmett drove first, but they would take turns driving.

The highway was close to their home. Emmett picked up speed and merged into the traffic. Maisie turned on the radio and blared the music. When either one of them had something to say, Maisie turned the radio volume down a notch. Emmett and Maisie were wearing their sunglasses since the sun filled the morning sky. It was a long drive to their destination, but they had a great time together along the way.

The GPS led Emmett and Maisie to the front of their luxury hotel. It was on the beach. They used valet parking. The walkway was lined with palm trees, and their room had a view of the ocean.

Emmett and Maisie decided to give themselves their own hotel tour. They found the workout room, an indoor pool, a bar, and vending machines. A large glass door led to an outdoor pool. Wind chimes outside the glass door sounded peaceful. There was another bar in the pool area. Emmett and Maisie decided to take a seat and order drinks.

A waiter asked what they would like to drink. They asked for exotic mixed drinks, and they were served with small umbrellas. Their view was incredible. As they sipped their drinks, they looked at people swimming in the pool and people walking along the beach. Some were wading in the ocean, and there were several surfers.

Emmett and Maisie ate dinner at the hotel restaurant. A DJ was playing music by a dance floor. Emmett asked Maisie if she wanted to have a dance with him.

She said, "Yes, of course."

Emmett had never seen Maisie dance. She was a bit klutzy and seemed to only know one dance move. Emmett didn't have the heart to tell her that she wasn't that good at dancing. She seemed to be having the time of her life.

The DJ played a slow song, and Emmett and Maisie embraced and danced to the music. Maisie was much better at slow dancing.

During the fast-paced songs though, Emmett stole the show. People gathered around the dance floor to watch Emmett dance. Maisie felt a bit jealous when several beautiful women began staring at him. Emmett noticed too, but he didn't make it obvious. Maisie was a bit worried that Emmett would find them more attractive. She didn't realize that Emmett was totally committed to her—and he was a completely loyal man.

Maisie sat back down at the table, and Emmett followed her.

"Are we done dancing for the night," Emmett asked.

"Those women were drooling over you. I had enough of it," she said.

Emmett laughed until he saw that Maisie was hurting inside. He took her hand and assured her that no one would ever get in the way of their relationship. Emmett and Maisie decided to return to their hotel room for the night.

After Emmett and Maisie woke up, they went for a continental breakfast. They were able to sit outside. It was warm outside, and the birds came close to their table for food. Everything was so different from their hometown. It was the perfect place for their vacation.

The concert was the next day, but in the meantime, they shopped. There were cute novelty shops and restaurants to visit. Emmett and Maisie held hands almost the entire time. They gave a tourist Maisie's phone and asked him to take a picture. It was perfect. They stood by a palm tree, and the wind blew Maisie's long hair. They were wearing sunglasses and summer clothing.

That evening, Maisie and Emmett viewed the most beautiful sunset above the ocean. It was so picturesque. Emmett turned toward Maisie and gave her a big hug and kiss. "Thank you. This has been the best trip I have ever been on."

The following day, Maisie and Emmett wandered around the hotel and visited an art museum. They spent two hours catching up on sleep and got ready for the concert.

CHAPTER 26

Maisie drove to the concert. It was a short trip from the hotel. They were both excited to see the show. When they arrived, people in orange shirts were directing traffic in the parking lot. One of the people was collecting the parking money. Maisie forgot to include small costs such as that in the vacation budget, but Emmett had no problem chipping in. As Maisie looked for parking money, Emmett reached over and paid the fee.

"Thanks, honey," she said.

"Not a problem," Emmett responded.

The walk to the stadium was long. Many other people were walking with them. When they reached the gate, Emmett handed the guard the tickets and was handed back the ticket stubs.

Inside the stadium, the seats were mostly taken. The sports stadium was also used for concerts. They sat on metal benches. Emmett and Maisie walked up twenty rows to get to their seats. Maisie sat on the end of the row, but Emmett sat between Maisie and a woman who was extremely loud. Her body frame was large, but her weight was size proportionate. It was apparent to everyone that she had been drinking too much. She was there with a group of ten people. Maisie hoped that the group would not be too loud and unruly. Emmett, however, was not concerned.

A band was playing ahead of the main attraction. They sounded really good, but Emmett and Maisie had never heard of them. Maisie commented to Emmett that they would probably end up making it big in the music world. Emmett agreed.

The weather was absolutely perfect. The air was warm with a slight breeze. It was dark outside, but the stadium lights lit up the entire place. Emmett's favorite band walked on stage. There were guitarists, a keyboard player, a drummer, and the lead singer. They started by playing Emmett's favorite song. Maisie turned to Emmett and joked that she had talked to the band ahead of time to arrange that. He laughed and continued to enjoy the band.

Maisie was able to capture some of the performance on video. She used her phone for the video and several pictures. Emmett was absorbed with listening to the band's performance. He wasn't concerned with pictures and videos, but he was happy Maisie was doing it for him.

A man in a baseball cap, glasses, a lightweight jacket, and jeans walked up the stadium steps. He paused two steps below Emmett and Maisie's seats and looked in their direction. His eyes focused on Maisie.

Emmett thought something was abnormal about the situation.

Maisie knew immediately that he was the man who she had pointed out to the FBI.

Hawk turned around and walked down the steps. Maisie thought he had purposely walked up the steps to look at them. It was too loud in the stadium to whisper, so Maisie texted Emmett's phone that he was the man who was after her.

Emmett texted: "Remain cool. We're not going to make a scene by leaving now. As soon as the concert is over, we'll get out of here."

Maisie thought they should leave immediately. She texted him and said she thought she should report him to the police now.

Emmett had already alerted the police, but he texted: "Later."

After the concert, Emmett and Maisie walked to Maisie's car and headed back to the hotel.

Maisie said, "Shouldn't we contact the police now?"

Emmett said they would call when they were back at the hotel.

When they got to their room, Emmett told Maisie that she could call the police. Maisie called, and the police said they would follow up with her later.

Maisie felt scared, but Emmett comforted her. He assured her that everything would turn out all right. He turned on the television, and they relaxed for the night.

CHAPTER 27

Hawk was part of a crime ring. The FBI had been working on the case for years. The crime ring was nearly shut down. They had everyone involved in custody except the ringleader—Hawk. The FBI immediately sent a team to track down Hawk. They were grateful for Emmett's tip.

The FBI and the police had been informed of Hawk's presence on the West Coast. He had been placed on the most wanted list that day. Hawk was considered armed and dangerous. The search for him was broadcast on every news station.

Hawk was driving a stolen vehicle. He knew the police were on his trail. He drove back roads toward the Mexican border. His power in the crime world had dissipated. Most of his connections were already jailed, which made it harder to escape.

Hawk was running low on gas. He knew he had no choice but to stop at a gas station. He stopped in a rural area to fill the gas tank, but he was spotted and reported to the police.

After he pulled out of the gas station, he headed south down a long country road. Two police cars quickly approached behind his car. He knew they were on his trail. Hawk kicked his car into high gear and sped down the road. As the police followed, more police cars appeared. Hawk made it to a main highway and headed south. By then, more than ten police cars were chasing him.

Suddenly, Hawk's car got a flat tire and began spinning. The police had put a spike strip on the highway and blocked off the roads to other traffic. Hawk's car stopped, and he began running.

Several police officers followed him on foot. Hawk's path was blocked by a wire fence. He jumped over it and continued into a wooded area. He remained in view of the police.

One of the police officers was able to get ahead of him from a different direction. Hawk just about ran right into the officer's path. Hawk looked stunned when he saw the officer. Just then, the other officers got close enough to grab him and push him to the ground. Handcuffs were placed on his wrists, and he was then taken into custody. The criminal ring had been brought to a final end.

CHAPTER 28

A year after Hawk was taken into police custody, the FBI closed the case. Hawk and the others from the crime ring were sentenced to federal prison for twenty-five years and more.

There had been talk inside FBI headquarters about Maisie and her role in the witness protection program. Now that the case was closed, her safety was no longer at risk. A special meeting was held at headquarters for all the agents involved in Maisie's case. It was led by Agent Miller who had been given information by his superiors to share at the meeting.

After all of the agents were seated in the conference room, Agent Miller stood in the front of the room and said, "Welcome and good morning. I have asked you all to be here so that I may make you aware of a decision made by my superiors in the Brooke Alden/Maisie Lexington witness protection program case. It is with rare exception that I am here to tell you that Brooke Alden/Maisie Lexington will be given the option to remain living her current life with no contact from anyone in her past or going back to her old life and family. The Federal Bureau of Investigation has come to the decision that Brooke Alden/Maisie Lexington is no longer in danger—and that returning to her old life would not put her or anyone else at risk."

The agents were then given the opportunity to ask Agent Miller questions. They had dozens of questions. The last question was about when Maisie would be notified of her choice.

Agent Miller said that he would contact Maisie immediately after the meeting; he hoped to be able to meet with her within a day or two.

That afternoon, the police arrived at Harvest Moon and spoke to Maisie.

Maisie told them that she could meet Agent Miller after her shift. The police arranged to pick her up and drive her to headquarters. She left her car in the parking lot, and the police drove her to FBI headquarters. Maisie made sure to let Emmett know that she would be coming home late.

CHAPTER 29

Agent Miller spent an hour with Maisie after he informed her about her options.

She looked at Agent Miller is complete shock. It had never entered her mind that this opportunity would present itself. She had never heard of it being done before.

Agent Miller stated that his precinct had never done anything like it.

For a few moments, Maisie absorbed the information.

Agent Miller told her to take a few days before making a final decision.

Maisie spent the next twenty-four hours trying to make her decision. She came to the conclusion that she would like to return to her old life and bring Emmett with her. That would mean that she'd have to inform Emmett about her old life. Emmett had only known Maisie's current life; anytime Emmett asked anything about her past, Maisie had to lie to him.

The following evening, Maisie told him the truth.

Emmett said his stomach didn't feel well, and he left the room. He returned thirty minutes later, looked at Maisie, and said, "You liar. You're nothing but a liar. You led me on. You lied about everything. I love you. How could you do this to me?"

The heated argument went on for fifteen minutes. Emmett said she could stay in the house for another week, but he would be spending the week in a motel. He wanted nothing to do with her—even though he was still deeply in love with her. Emmett packed a few things and went to a motel.

CHAPTER 30

After the argument with Emmett, Maisie thought she'd be better off returning to her old life. She knew that major change was not easy—and she really missed her mom, dad, siblings, and friends.

Maisie and Emmett broke up. Emmett was angry that Maisie had not told him about her true identity from the start.

Maisie decided to return to her old life. She informed Agent Miller the following day and was set to return home. Her family had been notified that she would be returning. They were given full details of her disappearance. Maisie's family was relieved that she was still alive. For two years, they had wondered if she was dead or alive. Her family was ecstatic. They could barely wait for the following day, but Maisie's dad had died the prior year on October 23.

Maisie thought of leaving without saying good-bye to anyone. She thought it might be too difficult on everyone. She decided it was best to say her good-byes to the closest people in her life. Besides, they had already been informed by the FBI that Maisie was no longer in danger.

Right after she informed Agent Miller about her decision, he instructed his staff to brief everyone involved in Maisie's secret life that she was leaving the area and heading home to her real family.

CHAPTER 31

Maisie was distraught and heartbroken. It was Thursday, and she had an appointment with Dr. Stockton. They talked about her decision for forty-five minutes.

Maisie told Dr. Stockton about her breakup with Emmett. He said she looked sad, but seeing her old family was such a great opportunity for her. Over time, she would heal. Dr. Stockton told Maisie that he would connect her with a new doctor. She would need a psychiatrist to aid in her transition back to Brooke, and he felt that she needed medication to help with the changes.

Dr. Stockton told her that he enjoyed being her doctor and that she would be missed. He wished her the best of luck.

She said, "Thank you. Good-bye."

CHAPTER 32

It was time for Maisie to say good-bye to the people who were close to her. She was still living in Emmett's house, but she had not heard anything from him. She would be leaving the next day.

Maisie thought the most important visit was Bob and Donna. They knew about her decision. Maisie drove to their house and saw Dominick's truck in the driveway. She rang the doorbell, and Bob and Donna welcomed her inside.

Dominick was there with Jillian and the kids. Robin and Edison ran up to her and gave her a big hug. They had always called her Aunt Maisie. Maisie didn't think leaving would have a big effect on her emotions, but she felt a tear in her eye.

Jillian walked over to her and hugged her. "We're going to miss you, Maisie."

"I'll miss everyone too," Maisie replied.

Bob and Donna stepped in and gave her a hug. Donna was sobbing. Maisie didn't realize how much of an impact she had made. "Thank you for taking me into your home and accepting me as part of your family."

Bob said, "It was our pleasure, Maisie."

Maisie had no idea it was going to be so hard to leave.

Charlie and Amanda arrived. They had been informed about the situation and Maisie's true identity the day before. They gave their word that they would not say anything to anyone until it was public information.

Amanda and Maisie hugged, tears streamed down Maisie's face. "I'll miss my best friend."

Charlie gave Maisie a hug and told her that she had been a good employee and that she would be greatly missed.

Everyone stayed at Bob and Donna's house for several hours. Bob took down the rope from the living room, sat down at the piano, and played several songs for Maisie.

Before everyone left, they said good-bye to Maisie once again.

Maisie returned to Emmett's house, packed her things, and wrote a thank-you note.

CHAPTER 33

A secret agent escorted Maisie during her trip. This arrangement was made as a precaution but was set to cease as soon as she arrived back home. As Maisie was about to ring the doorbell, the door flew open. Her family was greeting her as though it was an important birthday. Old friends were there—as well as family and distant relatives. A big sign said, "Welcome Home Brooke."

Her mother was first to give Maisie a big hug. She almost didn't let go. Tears rolled down her mother's face, but Maisie felt a bit numb. It was overwhelming and amazing at the same time. She hugged everyone who was there. One person was missing though—and she was aware of it. She looked at her brother and asked, "Where's Dad?"

Jeb stared back at her with a serious look.

She knew the answer was not going to be good. "Brooke, he died. Dad had a heart attack about a year ago."

Brooke no longer felt numb. A tear rolled down her face. "Was it a sudden death—or did he suffer?"

Jeb replied, "It was a massive heart attack, Brooke. He held on for a week."

Brooke nodded.

"Here. Dad wanted you to have this." Jeb handed Brooke a black crystal.

Brooke was stunned. "The mysteries of life," she muttered.

"What?" Jeb said.

"Oh nothing." Brooke thought about what the old woman at the store had said: "The mysteries of life—never forget they exist."

Brooke's mother approached her and said, "If this is all too much for you, I can ask them to leave."

Brooke said, "No, they can stay. It's good to see everyone."

A month went by, and Brooke settled back into her old life. She was unhappy and heartbroken. She missed Emmett. She also missed her southern family. She felt empty inside. Returning to her old life was not as glamorous as she had thought it would be.

Her phone lit up with Emmett's name. With excitement, she immediately answered.

Emmett asked how she was and asked how the adjustment was going.

Brooke poured her heart out and told him how much she missed him.

Emmett said he missed her too.

A few weeks later, Emmett arrived in the North to be with Brooke. When they were finally together, Emmett said, "I have a surprise for you. Pack your things."

"Why? Where are we going?" Brooke asked.

"Niagara Falls."

Brooke packed her belongings, and they drove to Niagara Falls. Since they didn't have passports, they stayed on the American side.

Emmett bent down on one knee and pulled a box out of his pocket. The other tourists were minding their own business.

When he opened the box, Brooke was completely stunned. She was shaking.

Emmett said, "Will you marry me?"

"Yes," Brooke said with no hesitation.

The two smiled at each other and hugged. While Emmett and Brooke embraced, Brooke turned her head to the side. Without intending to, she made quick eye contact with a male tourist. It reminded her of Hawk and the crime she had witnessed. She looked away as fast as she could and looked into the eyes of Emmett. They kissed again.

Brooke and Emmett married and lived the rest of their lives with contentment and love.

The phone rang at FBI headquarters, and Agent Adams picked it up. "Adams speaking."

"Sir, this is Agent Sullivan. I have important information in the Brooke Alden case."

"How is Brooke Alden doing these days, Sullivan?"

Agent Sullivan said, "Still in a coma, sir. Poor thing. Escaping from abuse and gets shot in an alley on her way to safety. Such a shame. We have a strong lead about the person involved in her shooting. Someone who goes by the name of Hawk."

ABOUT THE AUTHOR

Carolyn's childhood dreams were to become a mother and an author. After receiving her associate's in applied science degree from Monroe Community College, she began writing poetry. Two years later, writing was put on the back burner to focus on her career at Eastman Kodak Company and eventually motherhood. She is the proud mother of three grown children. Carolyn resides in Canandaigua, New York. As the survivor of domestic violence, she looks to be a role model and inspire others through her writing.

www.ingramcontent.com/pod-product-compliance
Lightning Source LLC
LaVergne TN
LVHW091546060526
838200LV00036B/720